The ancient mole city of Molanium is suffering from some invisible sickness which makes the molefolk weary all the time. Jason, a young mole, sets out to find a cure for his people accompanied by Oliver, an owl, and the two cats, Calico and Topaz. Before the quest is accomplished, many perils must be overcome and many adventures must be experienced in search of essential clues.

JASON'S QUEST

JASON'S QUEST

MARGARET LAURENCE

ILLUSTRATED BY STAFFAN TORELL

Alfred · A · Knopf / New York

THIS IS A BORZOI BOOK

PUBLISHED BY ALFRED A. KNOPF, INC.

Copyright © 1970 by Margaret Laurence

Illustrations © 1970 by Staffan Torell

All rights reserved under International and Pan-American Copyright Conventions.

Published in the United States by Alfred A. Knopf, Inc., New York, and

simultaneously in England by Macmillan & Co. Ltd., London,

and McClelland and Stewart, Ltd., Toronto, Canada.

Distributed by Random House, Inc., New York.

Library of Congress Catalog Card Number: 78–106138

Manufactured in the United States of America

For my friends:

Max, Ian, Leslie, and Steven Cameron

Contents

JASON'S QUEST

(1)

MOLANIUM,

THAT MIGHTY CITY

The great and noble city was in danger of its life. There was no doubt in Jason's mind about that. Sad and troublesome days had fallen upon Molanium. The city was dwindling and shrinking, growing smaller and shabbier every season. Even the Venerable Mole admitted that at no time in the history of the molefolk had the situation looked so grim. The trouble was that no one really knew what the trouble was. The moles had in the past been a sturdy, stalwart folk, always ready to work, or to sing when work was over, but now many of them seemed to be suffering from an invisible sickness which made them constantly weary and uncaring. Jason himself was one of the few who had not so far been affected, and he was worried, deeply worried.

"If the Venerable Mole and the Old Ones can't discover the

cause and the cure," he reflected, "how under earth can I? But someone's got to try."

Jason decided to go, as he often did, up to the outer world where he could be alone in the night and where the cool air might clear his head. He hoped his mother would not discover his absence, for Calpurnia worried whenever he left Molanium. True, the hazards of the outer world were many: cats, owls, weasels, foxes, and humans, to name only a few. Had not Jason's own father met an unfortunate fate up there? Calpurnia never tired of pointing out that very few moles these days ever ventured *Thither,* and those who did were considered madly reckless. "Thither" was the name the molefolk gave to the outer world. The Venerable Mole had explained once to Jason that the word implied dangers and perils, which should be avoided by all sensible moles. To Jason, however, Thither always seemed beckoning and mysterious, as though it were waiting to be discovered. But he never told anyone of this feeling.

Jason emerged from the Great North Tunnel and sniffed carefully. No smell of danger anywhere. Only the dark sweetness of the evening air and the far-off perfume of roses from the Pink Jungle some distance away. The jungle itself was forbidden territory for moles, as the Old Ones considered it to be too far from any access tunnel and also to be a favorite lurking place for ferocious cats. But Jason, after many nights of secretive tunneling, had dug his own escape burrow. It was not large, and it did not join up to any of the official tunnels, but it was large enough for him to scoot into, if any crisis arose. It lay in the very heart of the Pink Jungle, and this place, more than any other, fascinated Jason. The climbing roses grew in a tangle high above Jason's small, sleek, black head. When he looked up through the green nets of the leaves and branches to the huge, heavy-hanging clusters of blossoms, pinkish-white and whitish-pink, the colors mingling and pale in the light of the stars, his heart thumped excitedly, and he felt almost dizzy at the sight of the flower forest. He could not have explained how he felt about the Pink Jungle, so he never tried. He did not think that any other mole felt that way, and he had no desire to be laughed at by those of his own age, or scolded by his elders for foolhardiness in venturing so far. *Foolhardiness,* the Venerable Mole was fond of saying, *is for fools, but caution is for moles.*

Remembering the old mole's earnest voice now, Jason felt a slight uncertain queasiness in his insides. Probably something terrible would happen to him tonight, and serve him right. He skittered swiftly across the grass, realizing how vulnerable he was

5

on the open landscape and, by the time he reached his own special observation post in the Pink Jungle, he was breathing heavily with exhaustion and fright.

He had hardly recovered his breath and composure when he heard a noise that terrified him all over again. The *swish-swish-swoop* of wings in the night. Jason was just about to make rapidly for his escape burrow when he heard the voice.

"Hello there, mole. What are you doing here all by yourself?"

The tawny owl was by no means a large one. He was, in fact, almost a midget as owls went, and apparently quite young. Nevertheless, he was somewhat bigger than Jason, and he had claws and a sharp beak. *Courage,* Jason said to himself. What he actually felt, however, was not courage, but fear.

"Don't get in a panic," the owl went on, "I'm not a mole-eater, myself. Fact is, I'm not what you'd call a marvelous hunter of any sort. Insects, yes. But moles, now—moles never appealed to my hunting instincts."

"I'm delighted to hear it," Jason murmured, still shivering inside his fur.

"*You* may be delighted," the owl said, "but for me it's a disaster."

"Why?" Jason asked, his curiosity beginning to get the better of his fear.

6

"Because I'm not the way all reasonable owls are supposed to be," the owl replied. "It worries me. Not the hunting part, so much, but all the rest."

"I don't follow you very well," Jason admitted. "What do you mean—all the rest? By the way, my name's Jason."

"Glad to meet you, Jason," the owl said, extending a wingtip, which Jason slightly and cautiously touched with his paw. "I'm Oliver. My mother named me after Oliver Cromwell, in the hope that I might become a mighty leader. What hope she had, poor soul. I've been a tremendous disappointment. What comes into your head first when you think of owls?"

"Danger," Jason said instantly.

"No, no," Oliver said, sounding offended. "Maybe *you* think that, as a mole, but most creatures when they think of owls, think of wisdom. Owls are supposed to be wise. *The wise old owl.* Haven't you ever heard that saying? Well, the sad fact is that I'm not. Not wise, I mean. Not in the slightest."

"You seem quite sensible to me," Jason remarked.

"It's very kind of you to say so, Jason, and I appreciate it, but, well, I mean to say, as a mole you naturally would think I was sensible just because I'm not trying to grab you for my next meal, wouldn't you? That is, I don't feel you are really speaking about my finer qualities, if any—my intelligence, for example. Are you?"

7

"I consider you as my friend," Jason said impetuously.

Oliver turned his head slightly and raised one wingtip to conceal the fact that he was touched by this statement. "Well, so do I," he replied. "I consider you my friend, as well. Shall I tell you something, Jason? In strict confidence, of course."

"Oh, strict," Jason promised, crossing his heart with his right paw.

"I have it in mind," Oliver said dreamily, flickering his wings a little, as though contemplating flight, "I have it in mind to go on an expedition. More in the nature of a search, really. A quest."

"A quest? What are you looking for?"

"Well, for wisdom, actually," Oliver admitted, half embarrassed. "I don't feel I'm getting much wiser hanging around here. The likelihood of my turning into a wise old owl someday seems pretty remote to me, to tell you the truth, unless I do something about it. So I've been thinking—what about looking around elsewhere? I must be able to discover a few shreds and tatters somewhere, flotsam and jetsam of the mind. In other words, that is to say, wisdom, if you see what I mean. Sounds rather vague, I imagine."

Jason, who was not accustomed to such a talkative companion, nodded and tried to sort out exactly what Oliver had been saying. It seemed to him that the two of them had much in common.

8

"I—I—" he stammered a little, in his anxiety to avoid making himself sound foolish, "I've been thinking, in a way, of something of the sort, myself."

"You have?" Oliver cried. "What a coincidence! What are you interested in looking for?"

Jason thought for a moment. Words did not come as easily to him as they did to Oliver.

"A cure," he said finally.

"A cure? For what?"

"For whatever it is that's the matter with Molanium. The great city, you know. The underground city of the moles. The history of Molanium goes back, you see, in an unbroken line to Roman times. It was established soon after Caesar's conquest of Britain, and it has continued in honor and dignity ever since."

"You sound like a lecture," Oliver put in. "Not that it's boring, of course. On the contrary—very interesting. Do go on."

"I guess it *is* a lecture," Jason admitted. "It's not my own words. It's what every molechild learns by heart. Anyway, Oliver, something awful has happened. A strange disease has struck Molanium, and no one knows exactly what its cause is, or what to do about it."

"Symptoms?" Oliver inquired.

"The city is shrinking," Jason explained, "because new tunnels aren't getting built and the old tunnels aren't being properly looked after. The tunnels are being neglected because the Diggers and Delvers Guild is not getting enough new apprentices. And the reason for that seems to be that the molefolk are suffering from this unnamed disease which makes most of them feel terribly tired all the time. Bone-weary. Too exhausted to lift a shovel. Oliver, do you think it could be some sort of plague?"

"I'm not a medical man," Oliver said quickly. "Do they die of it?"

"In a way, they do. Our Master Physicians can't find any evidence of blights, sores, fever, or spots, but the mole people are dying younger than they used to, just dying for no apparent reason, from something invisible. Not a cheery thought, is it?"

"Far from cheery," Oliver agreed. "But what can you hope to discover, Jason?"

"I don't know," Jason said dejectedly. "I don't really know at all. But something tells me I have to try. There must be a cure somewhere. There must be someone who knows about this sort of thing. Look here—why don't you come down to Molanium and have a look for yourself? You might be able to make a few suggestions."

"Me?" Oliver screeched. "Me, go underground! Alone in a whole city of moles? Not on your life!"

"It's all right," Jason said, smiling. "I'll look after you. I know how we can avoid meeting anyone. At least, I think I do. Anyway, they'd be frightened of you."

"It would be mutual," Oliver said, fanning himself with a wingtip. "Well, if you really think it would be all right, maybe I'll go. I always wondered what it was like down there."

So across the rolling grass plains of the landscape they went, Jason scurrying and Oliver flying. But once they got inside the Great North Tunnel, it was Oliver who was at a disadvantage. He squeezed himself as small as he possibly could, and waddled along gingerly, but every few paces he nearly got stuck.

"Whew!" he gasped. "Up there I'm a dwarf, practically. But down here I'm a giant. We'll never make it, Jason."

"Patience," Jason said. "We'll soon be through the tunnel and out into the Low Street. From there, it's only a short scamper to the Old Ones' Council Room. We'll go there because it'll be empty at this time of night. I'm sorry I can't take you home to meet my mother, but it might be a little upsetting for her."

"Indeed it might," Oliver puffed. "You know, Jason, what surprises me? All the fresh air in this tunnel. I would have thought it would be quite stuffy, but it's not."

"Oh, we have air vents every so often," Jason explained, "and they pipe in the fresh air. They're very strongly constructed, and concealed even more carefully than the tunnel entrances. Our building practice is extremely sound, you know. We learned it from the Roman moles who found their way to this country with the first of the legions. They were great engineers, the Romans, and we are proud to count them among our forebears."

Then they were there. The Old Ones' Council Room or, to give it its proper name, The Great Council Hall of the Elders of Molanium, was a large and imposing room, at least by mole standards.

"At last!" Oliver cried, taking a deep breath and fluffing out his chest feathers.

"Sh," Jason whispered. "All except the Old Ones are expected to be quiet in here. This is a venerable place."

"I'm not certain," Oliver observed, "that I really know what *venerable* means."

"Well, it means—" Jason hesitated, not being all that certain himself, "I think it means very old and respected. This Council Hall is the oldest part of Molanium. It was here that Horatio, the noble founder of our city, tunneled and made his first camp. He was a Roman military mole, the mascot of the standard bearer of the Seventh. Gathering about him a loyal band of some nine or ten military moles, he charged off boldly to make his own conquest of Britain. Their first outpost was the beginning of the great city of moles. The Council Hall, although now much expanded, is in a sense a shrine to Horatio and his comrades-in-arms. You can still see his carved message on the wall. Look, Oliver, way up there. . . ."

Oliver craned his neck, and finally located some rather crooked and very tiny letters scratched on the wall.

HORATIO ERAT HIC

"Now you can see what I mean about not being wise," Oliver sighed. "I have to admit I can't read a word of Latin, Jason."

"Well, neither can I," Jason said consolingly. "I only know what it means because we were all taught it when very young. It says 'Horatio Was Here.' The ancient inscription is preserved carefully because it is our most precious relic."

"I had no idea," Oliver said, "that you moles were so keen on history and that."

"The Venerable Mole is always telling us: *Don't forget. We moles are the keepers of the traditions. That is the role of the mole.* Look, history all around us, Oliver," Jason said earnestly.

Oliver looked, and it was true. The Great Council Hall, dim and shadowy, was full of curious objects and ancient slogans chiseled into the hard-packed earth walls which resembled dull red brick and glowed faintly in the gray glimmering light that

13

filtered in from the air shafts. At the front of the hall was a raised platform, upon which stood the throne of the Venerable Mole, dark brown polished oak, high-backed and elaborately carved with twisting earthworms, with a background of grasses and leaves. Beside the Venerable Mole's chair stood the standard of Horatio with its marvelously lifelike woodcarving sheathed in thin-beaten precious metal—The Golden Mole of the Seventh.

The rest of the Council Hall was filled with the sedate and ornate chairs of the elders, each with its own family motto; *Haste Is Idiocy, Bank Your Fires, Slow—Danger Ahead,* and so on.

On the front wall hung a large tapestry, an exquisite work in subdued tones of blue and rose, purchased, as Jason explained, at vast expense from the moles of Bayeux, France, and depicting the later life and times of Sir Alain de Molyneux, the bloodthirsty Norman mole who had laid siege to Molanium at the time of William the Conqueror. The passing of the years, fortunately, had gentled Sir Alain and his followers, and the tapestry showed them dancing around the beribboned Mole Pole on May Day, while flutists fluted and mole maidens threw camomile flowers.

Oliver and Jason examined the cleverly wrought mottoes and slogans which decorated the other walls. The largest was done in scrolled and bedizened lettering, colored in gold and crimson.

FESTINA LENTE

"The ancient motto of the molefolk," Jason said. "It means *Hurry Slowly*."

"I don't see how one *could* hurry slowly," Oliver commented. "I mean, that wouldn't really be hurrying, would it?"

"I know," Jason said in an exceedingly low voice, glancing around as though to make sure they were truly alone. "I've had

15

that thought sometimes, too. But I wouldn't want the Old Ones to know."

"Why ever not?"

"Well," Jason said uncomfortably, "It would be frowned on, that's all. Don't let's talk of it now. Look, there's one of the most highly valued inscriptions in the whole Council Hall. It dates back to the Middle Ages."

Slowly, Oliver read the gilt and blue words.

They who think ye worlde not flat,
Deserve to be consumed by cat.

"I don't want to seem squeamish, Jason," he said, "but it's rather gruesome, isn't it?"

"The lettering," Jason felt it his duty to remark, "is said to be splendid."

"Yes, but Jason . . ."

"Mm?"

"The world's *not* flat," Oliver observed. "I know I'm not very wise, but I do know that. The world is round."

Jason glanced around again, apprehensively. "Sh," he said at last. "We know, too. But . . ."

"But *what?*"

"Well, it's not considered good manners to *say* it. You know."

Oliver was mystified. "No, I don't know."

"Never mind," Jason said and shrugged. "I—I can't explain. I don't really understand it very well myself. It has something to do with the inscriptions being venerable, I think. And our not making rude remarks about the ancestors. Look, Oliver, just over here, that plaque is in memory of my own father."

Oliver looked and read:

Alas, poor Harold, mark him well.
He met a cat without a bell.
He stood his ground, and sad to tell,
His courage caused his funeral knell.

"Why, that's heroic!" Oliver cried in admiration.

"I think so, too," Jason said warmly. "Although it's actually meant as a dreadful warning."

"I don't wonder that you have a quest in mind," Oliver said. "I expect you come by it naturally. You've probably inherited your father's bravery."

"Oh, Oliver . . ." Jason said longingly. "If only that were true. But it isn't. I'm afraid of millions of things."

Just then, there was a swishing sound and the rustle of robes. Then a faint and elderly cough. Jason and Oliver swung around, appalled, and there in the doorway of the Council Hall stood a bent and very aged mole in spectacles and what appeared to be a dark red velvet dressing gown.

"Jason, of course," the Venerable Mole pronounced in a creaking and yet immensely stern voice. "Who else? Who else troubles and distracts my advancing years? Who else would be found within the sacred Council Hall, completely without reason or permission, and accompanied by an outsider, an enemy from Thither, and—if I am not greatly mistaken—a member of the notorious and noxious owl race?"

Jason trembled and stuttered. "It's—he's—n-n-not really an owl, sir. He's Oliver. That is, he's an owl, b-but he's questing. Like me. That is—um—what I mean is . . ."

Oliver, after trying unsuccessfully to crouch behind one of the Old Ones' chairs, which was much too small and failed to conceal his jutting wingfeathers, decided he had better try to explain.

"Don't blame Jason, sir," he said, "I wanted to see Molanium, and I promise you that I'm not a hunting kind of owl."

"That is what *you* say, young fellow," the Venerable Mole replied, frowning over his spectacles, "but I recall the old proverb of our people. . . ."

In a sonorous voice he quoted it:

Owls are the enemy.
Owls are the foe.
Owls mean danger.
Owls mean woe.

"Please, sir," Jason put in timidly, "may I say something?"

"I suppose so," the old mole said grudgingly. "What is it, Jason?"

"If Oliver was going to eat me, wouldn't he have done it already?"

"Hm," the Venerable Mole said. "You may have a point there. I don't say you *do*. I just say you may have. I shall have to consider it."

From the folds of his red velvet robe, the Venerable Mole drew forth a cap. It was mauve and green striped, long and pointed and slightly floppy, and on the peak of it there was a golden pompom. The Venerable Mole placed the cap carefully on his head, drawing it down snugly over his ears. He then turned his back on Jason and Oliver.

"Excuse me a moment, won't you?" he murmured.

"What *is* it?" Oliver whispered.

"Sh. It's the Cap Of Deeper Thinking. Very old. It's said to

19

possess magical powers. The Venerable Mole only uses it for extremely difficult problems."

"Oh," said Oliver. "Well, I don't wish to appear unreasonable, Jason, but it's not very nice to be called an Extremely Difficult Problem."

"I know, Oliver," Jason said sympathetically, "and I'm ever so sorry, but . . ."

Just then the Venerable Mole turned and faced them once more. "Your guess, Jason," he said, "is probably correct. Had this owl intended to make a meal of you, he would have done so already and would even now be rampaging through the city like a barbarian horde."

"What a thought," Oliver said peevishly. "As if I would."

"I do not suggest that his presence will be welcomed here for very long," the old mole continued. "That would not do at all. It might spread panic and chaos through the streets of Molanium. I will, however, allow him to remain for a further five minutes or so, until you can explain. What is all this wild talking about questing, Jason?"

So Jason explained, clasping and unclasping his paws in his nervousness. He told about Oliver's desire to go on a quest for wisdom in order to become as wise as all proper owls were meant to be, and he told of his own desire to search for a cure for the invisible sickness that was destroying Molanium and the molefolk.

The Venerable Mole listened in silence. Even after Jason had finished, the old mole did not say a word for a long time. Finally he sighed, and when he spoke, his voice was unexpectedly gentle.

"Jason, I have often scolded you for your pranks, but now you put me to shame. My boy, I have been hoping that someone would offer to go Thither and seek a remedy. I knew I could not go myself. I am too old and besides, I am needed here. The quest may be long, and the road may be filled with perils and deadly plights, with dangers, dragons, or demons. Who can tell? But I give you my blessing. I cannot do otherwise. Now see your owl friend out safely, and then make your preparations."

"Oh, sir . . ." Jason was overcome with emotion, and could say no more. He turned to go.

"Wait! One last thing," the Venerable Mole said. "Here, Jason. You will take the Cap Of Deeper Thinking with you. Wear it at all times. May it protect you and, in moments of great difficulty, may it help you to make wise decisions."

He placed the striped cap with its golden tassels on Jason's bowed head. Jason felt very young and small. It was a great occasion, calling for great words, but Jason had none.

"I—I will try," was all he could say.

"Who could say more?" the old mole said. "Spoken like a true mole, Jason."

Jason looked at the Venerable Mole in amazement. Had he, Jason, said the right thing after all? The Cap Of Deeper Thinking must be working already.

The old mole smiled a little, as though he could read Jason's thoughts. "The cap only works for those who already have some understanding, Jason. Now off with you before the morning comes."

Jason and Oliver quickly made their way up the deserted Low Street, into the North Tunnel, and up to the plains.

"Dusk tomorrow," Oliver said. "How does that sound as a time to begin?"

"Fine," Jason said. "Where shall we meet?"

Oliver had just begun to reply when they both heard voices. Loud voices. Mewing voices.

"Sh! Quick!" Oliver whispered. "Hide behind this rhododendron bush."

They swiftly concealed themselves, and listened and watched. There were two cats; a large dark cat whose silky fur had flecks of cream and gold colors in it, and a much smaller cat, prettily marked in white, black, and ginger. The big cat was sitting still on the grass. The little cat was dancing. The big cat was grumbling. The little cat was singing.

"Unfair, I call it," the big cat was saying. "Unfair to the whole cat species. Why, I ask you, is the cat always the villain? The children were looking at the cartoons on television today, so I went in and had a look. I thought it might be different this time, but oh no. I can't tell you how much they upset me. Time and time again, the same things happen. Poor little mouse chased by horrible huge cat. Clever little mouse fooling stupid giant cat. I ask you, Topaz, is it fair? Is it true? Is it kind?"

"Tra la la and hi di ho," the small cat trilled. "Around the rosebush we will go."

"Topaz, you're frivolous," the bigger cat said. "I don't believe you've been listening at all."

"You're too serious," Topaz replied. "Now, don't be annoyed, Calico. You know it's true. Too serious. Stuffy, one might almost say. Look! Don't you think I dance well? Don't you think I'm pretty?"

"You're vain, that's what *you* are," Calico said crossly. "I may not be your real aunt, little T, but I'm like an aunt to you, and it is my unpleasant duty to tell you, you are conceited and bird-brained."

"Piffle," Topaz said, continuing to dance. "Piffle and bosh. What're you, then, I should like to know? Perfect, I suppose."

"Certainly not," Calico said with dignity. "But at least I am concerned with important matters. What I would like to do,

Topaz, is a noble deed, to prove that cats are fine upstanding creatures."

Topaz stopped dancing. "Noble deed?" she inquired with interest. "What sort of noble deed?"

"That's the trouble," Calico said. "I don't really know."

In their hiding place behind the rhododendron bush, Oliver poked Jason. "Hear that? Now, watch me. You wait here." With that, Oliver flew out and up, hovering over the heads of the cats.

"Good evening," he said politely. "Now don't be surprised, please, and don't, for goodness sake, get any notions about chasing me. The fact is I couldn't help overhearing your talk and, as it happens, I think my friend and I can suggest an exceedingly noble deed which might appeal to you. If you agree to my plan, cats will probably be known as heroes or, in your case, heroines, forever more."

"For an owl, you are certainly very chatty," Calico said. "Well, all right. Let's hear your suggestion. I don't say I'll think much of it, mind."

"Promise not to hurt either my mole friend or myself?" Oliver insisted, still flapping around in the air.

"Oh, do let's promise, Calico!" Topaz cried. "I'm curious to know what noble deed we could do."

"Very well, then," Calico said. "I promise. A state of general amnesty shall be declared. That means no bashing, anyone."

24

Thus it was that the four met under the rhododendron bush on that momentous evening. When the two cats heard about the quest, they readily agreed to join it and to act as steeds for the other two, carrying them speedily from place to place, and helping them in moments of danger. Oliver, of course, would fly part of the time but, in order to save his strength and also not to get too far ahead of the others, he would ride two hours out of three.

"Whee! It's going to be fun," Topaz cried, running around in circles. "Look at me! I'm a steed! I'm a trusty charger! Half-a-league, half-a-league, half-a-league onward!"

"Do shut up," Calico said, "while we make plans. I think we should all understand one thing very clearly."

"What?" they all asked.

"That Jason is the leader of the expedition," Calico said.

"Me?" Jason said in astonishment. "Why me? I'm the smallest."

"You may be the smallest, my dear," Calico said in her practical voice, "but your purpose is the greatest. You want to save the molefolk and Molanium by finding a cure for the invisible sickness. So I think you should be the leader."

"Hear, hear!" Oliver shouted, clapping his wings.

Jason looked at his feet. Then he touched one paw lightly to the cap he was wearing, as though to give himself courage.

"Very well," he said at last. "I'll try."

25

"Well spoken," Calico said. "You do realize, though, don't you, that if you're captain, it means you have to give orders from time to time? Make decisions. Plan campaigns."

Jason had not really realized this at all, but he saw it now and nodded, hoping he looked reasonably confident, although inside he felt the opposite.

So it was arranged. They would leave the following evening, as soon as dusk fell, and they would take the road to a human city which Jason said he had heard about. He wasn't quite sure, but he thought its name was Londinium. They would not plan any further ahead. They would wait and see what happened.

"Four for one and one for four," Topaz sang. "Together till the journey's o'er."

"That's very good, Topaz," Jason said. "It will be our motto. Come on, let's all sing it."

They joined paws and wings, and stood in a circle, chanting the verse:

Four for One and One for Four,
Together till the journey's o'er.

Then they all went home to sleep the day through.

(2)

DRAGONS ARE NOT

WHAT THEY SEEM

Dusk finally arrived, and from the blue china clock on the mantel-piece, Jason knew that the gray light would have come to Thither and soon the night would descend with its blessed darkness which enabled the eyes of moles to see. The time of departure was near.

Jason looked around the cottage where he had lived all his life with his mother, Calpurnia, and his three sisters: Grace, Beauty, and Faith. He looked at the brick fireplace with its glowing coals, and at the brass teakettle hanging above on an iron hook. How many times had the old kettle boiled water for their evening tea, while the winter winds howled like ice demons away up Thither, and Grace, Beauty, and Faith perched on the sagging, green plush sofa sang *Molanium The Mighty, With Twenty Tunnels Blest* in three parts with harmony and descant? He would miss those evenings. He looked at the sampler hanging above the fireplace, done by his great-great-great-great grandmother when young, and embroidered with numerals one to ten as well as the alphabet and strange stiff birds in purple cross stitch. At the bottom of the sampler were the words *Posy M. Age twelve. 1754.* Jason said a silent good-bye to that distant relative, once age twelve. He looked at the big black spool table, brought here with difficulty through a specially made tunnel by his grandfather, and now polished until it shone like richest ebony. He looked at the sideboard where the cups were kept, the acorn cups for which his father had carved delicate handles in the shape of dandelions with curving stems. Jason looked at all these things and felt an ache in the area of his heart. Then he touched his paw to the Cap Of Deeper Thinking, and decided he must try to be cheerful.

"Come on, Jason," he told himself. "Time to go."

Calpurnia, rather tearful, but trying to hide it by fussing, handed him his shoulder bag.

"Now, luv, I've put in your warm socks for cold weather, and a packet of sunflower seeds in case of sudden hunger, and your handkerchief which you're not to forget to use when needed, and a needle and thread for mending purposes, and a bottle of liniment which you're to remember to rub on your feet in case of sore muscles and on your chest in case of sniffles, and . . ."

"I will—yes—I promise—please don't worry," Jason said.

His three sisters all had good-bye gifts for him. Grace gave him a slightly squashed gooseberry cake which she had made her-self. Beauty gave him some dried sage leaves and a red and white spotted handkerchief which she had sewn specially.

"The sage is to be brewed into a tea whenever you feel a cough coming on," she said, "and the handkerchief can be used as a flag."

Faith, being the youngest of the family, and still quite small, hadn't been able to think of anything clever to give to Jason, so she had just printed a farewell card for him. She had done it with great care on a strip of birch bark, and it said:

CUM HOMƎ SAFƎ

Jason thought he liked this present most of all, although he didn't say so, not wanting to hurt the others' feelings. He hugged Faith, thanked all of them, kissed his mother, and then, slinging on his shoulder bag, he was ready to go.

They stood and waved to him, and Jason waved back, until he rounded the corner and turned into the Low Street. Now he was really on his way. Along the street a few rheumatic old moles sauntered, poking idly with their canes at the discarded rubbish that littered the streets of Molanium these days. A few young moles lolled in doorways or snoozed on corners, most of them too lackadaisical to do more than feebly lift a paw in greeting as

Jason plodded past. The invisible sickness was everywhere. It saddened Jason to see it, and yet it made him all the more determined to find a cure—somehow, somewhere.

Emerging from the North Tunnel, Jason at once saw Oliver. The owl was flying around distractedly, looking upset.

"Oliver, whatever is the matter?" Jason asked.

"Oh, there you are," Oliver twittered. "Must say it's about time, too. Been here for *hours,* I have. Well, half an hour, anyway. What's been keeping you? I can't think where the others are. Never trust a cat, my Gran always says, but did I listen to her? Not I. And now those two have probably changed their minds.

How can we go on an expedition if nobody turns up at the proper time? I've never seen such unpunctuality in my entire life."

"Hush, hush," Jason said soothingly, trying not to smile. "You're just impatient, that's all. No one's late. Look! here they come now."

And sure enough, there were the two cats, Calico walking swiftly but with dignity across the grass, and Topaz prancing and skittering behind. Jason remembered all at once that he was supposed to be captain.

"Good," he said, trying to make his voice sound captainlike. "We're all here. Now let's have a last-minute check, shall we? Just to make sure we haven't forgotten anything."

"Very sensible," Calico agreed.

"I can't have forgotten anything," Topaz said, "for the simple reason that I'm not bringing anything. Just my own sweet self, that's all."

"Sh," Calico hissed, although not unkindly. "Can't you see that Captain Jason is checking supplies? That's an important matter."

Jason's paws shook a little. He had to admit to himself that he didn't feel much like captain. In fact, he felt decidedly nervous. But here he was, and he had to go on.

"Have we all got enough food, at least for the first night's march?" he asked.

"We've got a basket full of assorted goodies," Calico said. "Catnip, cold salmon, and some very sustaining biscuits. Or at least *I* have. Topaz was too busy finding a piece of velvet ribbon for her neck to do any worrying about provisions. Never mind. We can't all be practical, and I expect she'll be very good for light entertainment on the trip."

"How nice of you, Cal," Topaz purred. "You really are a pretty good old thing at heart, and I don't mean it for more than a minute when I call you stuffy."

Oliver could stand it no longer. "My heaven!" he shouted, expanding his chest feathers as he always did when annoyed. "Won't we ever get going? Talk, talk, talk—it will be midday before we go, and then Jason and I won't be able to see . . ."

He stopped short. "Oh-oh," he said abruptly.

"What is it?" Jason asked.

"Just remembered," Oliver said in some embarrassment. "I've forgotten something. Be back in a flash."

He zoomed off before Calico could point out (which she did anyhow) that she hoped he now saw the reason for a final checking of supplies.

In a few moments Oliver was back. On the tip of each wing he carried a pair of sunglasses, one pair slightly larger than the other, but both quite miniature.

"Here," he said as he thrust the smaller pair into Jason's

paws. "My Gran made them. I asked her to. Thought it would be a good idea. She's clever at making things, my Gran is. She found the bits of green glass in the deserted nest of a magpie— awful thieves, magpies. Look! The frames are made of very tough fibers from the creeper vines, stiffened with old hairpins she picked up on the path. Not bad, eh? It's so we can see properly, you know, Jason, if ever we have to travel during the day."

Jason was delighted. "Why, they're wonderful," he cried. "I wish I had something to give you, Oliver. Hang on a second, I know. My sister, Beauty, gave me a big red and white spotted handkerchief to use as a flag. As you're the one with wings, you can be our chief of signals. You can wave *All Clear Ahead* to us. Here—you keep it."

"Thanks *very* much," Oliver said gratefully. "Chief of signals, I like that. It has a nice ringing sound. Chief of signals."

As he handed the handkerchief to Oliver, Jason had a sudden premonition. Just a slight sinking feeling in the pit of his stomach. Something told him that Oliver would one day need the flag for a more dangerous purpose than waving All Clear Ahead. This did not seem the moment to mention any possible dangers, how- ever, so Jason hopped up on Calico's back and hung on firmly to the short reins she had made from two pieces of string. Then, at last, they started. The quest had begun.

Oliver, too excited to travel on the ground, decided to fly for a while. That left Topaz free to potter along however she wished, exploring the roadside and occasionally sneezing when she sniffed too deeply at a patch of buttercups and got the powdery pollen in her nose. As she cantered along, she sang:

> *Londinium, Londinium,*
> *That's where we're going in-ium.*
> *Oh, we don't give a pin-ium,*
> *For we all know we'll win-ium.*

Jason felt extremely happy. Nothing was settled, nothing was yet discovered, but it was good simply to be going somewhere, to be on the road to who-knows-what. They were still on a country lane. Later, they would have to travel on a highway where, according to Calico, who had once ventured that far, the traffic was terrible. But for the moment all was peace, and the hedges on either side glistened with the webs the spiders wove nightly. The wind was low and the branches of the beech and oak trees voiced only slight shushing whispers in the night. A cricket violined. A striped snake slithered. A toad plopped out of the grass and stared with unblinking jewel eyes at the travelers.

"You all right, Jason?" Calico inquired.

"Fine. I'm hoping Oliver hasn't gone too far ahead, though."

"No-o-o," came Oliver's whooing voice from above, and down he came, lighting gracefully on the furry neck of Topaz.

"Hey! Watch it!" Topaz shouted. "You frightened me. Anyway, I've changed my mind. I don't want to be a steed and trusty charger. It's more fun to prowl around by myself."

"Tough luck," Oliver said unfeelingly. "I've flown back and forth about a million times, trying not to get so far ahead that I'd lose you, and now I'm exhausted. So you're a trusty charger whether you like it or not."

"I'll shake you off into a blackberry bush, you bag of feathers!" Topaz threatened. "See if I don't."

Jason waited for Calico to scold the little cat, but Calico said nothing. Finally Jason realized what was expected.

"Now then, Topaz," he said, trying to make his voice stern, "we'll have no nonsense from you. You've had a good long time to explore the ditches. Every member of this expedition has to take some responsibility. Understand?"

To his surprise, Topaz mewed fairly meekly. "All right, Jason. No need to go on about it. Here, Oliver, catch hold of the ends of this ribbon around my neck."

"Well done, my dear," Calico said to Jason. Then, more loudly, "I forgot to tell you; I've brought along some coinage in case we need it."

"Coinage?" they all asked.

"Money," Calico explained. "Four silver threepennies I found one Christmas under the sofa and tucked away for a rainy day. They're rather rare now, you know, the silver ones, so they may be worth a good deal. I know we all tend to associate money only with humans, but we're heading for a human city, and you never know when these coins may come in handy."

"I think that's splendid, Calico," Jason said. "We'll call it the Silver Reserve, and only bring it out in times of dire need. I do wish we had a map, but I wasn't able to find a small one anywhere in Molanium. There was only the ancient scroll map in the Great Council Hall, and it was much too large and too precious to take away. It's a very old map, and maybe, I'm not sure, *maybe* it's a little out of date. I found Londinium on it, and lots of places marked *Fens and Swamps*. Some parts said *Here Be Dragons*. Do you think we shall encounter any dragons, Oliver?"

"Shouldn't think so," the owl reflected. "It's my impression that they all died out some time ago. Can't ever tell, though, can you? I must say I can't imagine what we'd do if we *did* meet a dragon, Jason. Can't quite see any of us slaying it, can you? In all honesty, now?"

"No," Jason admitted. "I can't, really. Still, perhaps we'd find we could, if we had to."

"If I met a dragon," Topaz put in, "I know exactly what I'd

do. I'd put on a terrific act. I'd snarl and show my teeth and act like a ferocious tiger, and the dragon would slink off to its home to hide."

At exactly that moment, there was a sharp sound of grass being stepped on, and a large something landed beside them on the lane. Jason squeaked; Oliver shrieked; Topaz yodelled in terror. Only Calico managed to conceal her fear.

"Good evening," the voice said courteously. "Sorry, I'm afraid I've startled you. I certainly didn't mean to. I spotted you a little while ago. I've been traveling in that field over there and I wanted to say hello, but I thought—well, I guess I thought you might not welcome company, so I hesitated to introduce myself. My name's Winstanley."

The strange cat was white with black markings on his ears, chest, and tail.

"I hope you don't mind my intruding like this," he went on. "If you do, then of course I'll push off immediately."

"Goodness, no," Calico said in her warm sensible voice. "Why should we mind? As long as you're considerate towards Jason, who is a mole and the captain of our group, and Oliver, who is an owl and our chief of signals, then you're welcome to travel along with us. I'm Calico and this is Topaz."

"Glad to meet you, one and all," Winstanley said. "It's most kind of you to let me share your company. I never used to think

I was all that talkative, you know, until I began this journey on my own."

"Yes," Calico agreed. "It must be extremely lonely. I know I wouldn't like it. Are you going far?"

"Far enough," Winstanley said with a faint smile. "What about you?"

"Oh yes," Calico said. "Tell him, Jason."

So Jason told him how the four of them had met, and why they were going on a quest, each for his own purposes; Oliver to look for wisdom, the cats to perform noble deeds, himself to find a cure for the mysterious illness that was causing the downfall of Molanium.

"I must say I admire you," Winstanley commented. "I think it's wonderful to be doing this sort of thing all on your own. Nobody forcing you to go, I mean. Your own free choice. It's courageous, and I certainly wish you luck."

"That's kind of you," Jason replied. "If it isn't a rude question, what is the purpose of your own journey?"

A sudden look of sadness crossed Winstanley's face. "Not a very cheerful one, I'm afraid. Better not to talk of it, perhaps. I don't want to depress you."

"Oh, do tell us," Topaz pleaded, her curiosity, as always, bubbling up at the slightest suggestion of a secret.

"Hush, Topaz," Calico commanded. Then, to Winstanley,

"Do as you think best, of course. But it might do you good to speak of it, if you've got troubles."

Winstanley sighed and for a moment was silent.

"You're right," he said finally. "I've been longing to tell someone. But you know how it is; one hates to burden others with one's own problems. The trouble, you see, is my son."

"Gone wrong, has he?" Calico inquired.

They were continuing their steady pace along the lane, but they had all become so interested in hearing Winstanley's story that they hardly noticed their surroundings.

"Oh, no," Winstanley said. "Nothing like that. No, he's stranded, that's the difficulty. Stranded in Africa. So that's where I'm headed. How I shall get there, I really don't know, but get there I must."

"Africa!" they all cried.

"Yes," Winstanley went on. "It may sound strange, but there he is. He's a good lad, is Samuel. Nearly grownup now, of course. So when he went to live with a human family who were going to Africa, I didn't object. His mother and I thought it would be a chance for him to see the world. He'd always been keen to travel, forever talking about far off countries, jungles and palm trees, that sort of thing. So off he went to Zanzibar. For a while all was well. We used to get post cards from him, saying how splendid Africa was. I think I've got one somewhere here."

Winstanley rummaged in his briefcase and brought out a postcard. On the front there was a color picture of a sandy beach, a blue-green sea, and a fleet of little fishing boats with billowing triangular sails. On the back was a stamp which said *Zanzibar,* and the following message:

> *Dear Dad and Mum:*
> *Hope this finds you as well as it leaves me.*
> *Africa is terrific. Went hunting today. Leopards,*
> *lions, elephants, and others too numerous to*
> *mention.*
>
>

Your loving son,

Samuel.

"My heavens," Oliver said in amazement, after they had all peered at the post card. "What a thrilling life!"

"Yes," Winstanley said bitterly, "it was thrilling all right. For a while. Then the terrible thing happened."

"A hunting accident?" Calico ventured.

"A dread tropical disease?" Jason asked, shuddering.

"Lion bit off his head, I expect. *Crunch!* All right, Cal, you needn't poke me like that." This from Topaz.

"No," Winstanley said. "Not any of those. Samuel's humans

moved away from Zanzibar and they left Samuel behind. Deserted him. Left him in the lurch. Turned him loose to fend for himself."

"Shame on them!" Calico cried, upset and outraged. "The poor cat-child. What did he do?"

"He tried to make his way back to England," Winstanley said. "He had it all arranged with an old seacat who lived on a British freighter, *The Dainty Dunce*. Young Samuel was to climb aboard the evening the ship set off from Zanzibar, and be a stowaway. The seacat had agreed to hide him in a lifeboat and to smuggle scraps of food to him. But just as Samuel was walking up one of the ropes that connected the ship to the dock, a sailor saw him and threw a ripe mango at him. Samuel, stunned by the mango, fell from the rope and hit the dock, breaking his two front legs."

They all groaned in sympathy, thinking of Samuel in such a state, so far from home.

"The old seacat sent a message when he got back to England," Winstanley finished, "so that is how I learned the awful news. Samuel may be dead by now, for all I know. But I'm determined to go and find out and, if he is still alive, I shall find some way of bringing him home."

"I think," Calico said, "that you're tremendously brave, Winstanley."

"But how are you going to get to Zanzibar?" Oliver asked.

"My plan is to work my way over on a boat," Winstanley said. "Galley cat, that sort of thing."

"Couldn't you fly?" Oliver persisted. "Much quicker, you know. Personally, I'm a great believer in flying. I've never had occasion to use artificial wings, of course, but I understand that planes are not at all bad, as far as imitations go."

"There's nothing I should like better than to go by air," Winstanley replied, "but I'm afraid it's impossible. Everything is very carefully checked at airports. There is no way of slipping aboard a plane without being noticed. And I don't have the money for a ticket. No, I've given a lot of thought to it and, as far as I can see, my only chance is to work my way by ship."

"If there's a quicker way of reaching your son," Calico said, "it seems a great pity that you can't take it."

"There! I knew I shouldn't have told you," Winstanley said apologetically. "Now you've begun to worry. Please don't. I shall get to Zanzibar, never fear."

Just then, rounding a bend in the road, they sighted a village ahead. Without their having realized it, the night was almost over. The sky was growing lighter, and in a short time the sun would be appearing over the fields at the edge of the horizon. Early birds were singing and beginning to bustle around in the tree branches.

"Town ahead," Oliver shouted, suddenly remembering that he was chief of signals. "Or should I say *Town Ahoy?*"

"*Ahoy* is only for ships, I think," Jason said. "What about staying here for the day? We've got to sleep somewhere and this looks like quite a nice place. I wonder what village it is? Do you happen to know, Winstanley?"

"No, I'm afraid I'm not familiar with this part of the country at all," Winstanley said. "Wait, though—isn't that a signpost?"

They looked, and there it was. *Stumbleton.*

The village was small but pretty, a collection of flint-and-brick cottages, some with thatched roofs and others with roofs of red slate. Each house had its well-kept garden, some favoring lavender, roses, and sweet-scented herbs such as rosemary and thyme, and others displaying tidy rows of plump green cabbages and fernlike carrot tops.

"I think we're in luck," Winstanley said. "Look! There's an inn. *The Dancing Monkey.* It's been my experience that wherever there's a human inn, the stable cat usually runs his own hostelry for us. Would you like me to nip in and find out? It might be as well for someone to explain about Oliver and Jason. Otherwise, if the place is full of farm cats having a noggin or two of ale, you never know what might happen."

"Why, that's very kind of you, Winstanley," Jason said. "We'd appreciate it."

Winstanley ran off, and in a few minutes he was back. "The coast is clear," he told them. "There's quite a good cats' inn in the old barn, where we can get a decent day's lodgings, and the innkeeper has promised that Jason and Oliver will be safe."

Soon they were all settled around the fireplace in the cats' inn. The innkeeper, a portly whiskered tom by the name of Bertrand, kept coming up and asking them if they were comfortable.

"Had enough to eat?" he asked Topaz. "We've got a little more of the haddock stew in the kitchen, if you fancy it."

"No, thanks," Topaz purred. "I'm full right up to bursting. No, I'm not supposed to say that. I'm supposed to say I've had an elegant sufficiency, and any more would be a super—super something."

"Superfluity," Calico told her. "That means too much, my dear. It's nice to see you paying attention to your manners."

"A little ale for you, sir?" Bertrand asked Jason. "Or some honey mead, if you prefer?"

"Nothing, thanks," Jason said. "You've been most hospitable, but I think we should all go to sleep now. We've got a long evening ahead tomorrow."

Jason, in truth, was tired out. So much had happened in such a short time, and he was not used to very much happening at all. In Molanium, whole weeks could pass with scarcely anything to remark upon, but here in Thither they had traveled the long road, met Winstanley, and come to the inn of The Dancing Monkey, where the farm cats jostled and joked and Bertrand bustled busily. Jason felt quite exhausted with all this activity.

When the four of them were by themselves in a loft filled with fresh soft hay, Calico announced that she couldn't sleep.

"It's Winstanley and his troubles," she said. "I can't get it out of my mind. You know what I've been thinking, Jason?"

"No," said Jason, although he thought he did, really.

"I've been thinking about our Silver Reserve," Calico said. "I know we were supposed to use it only for dire emergencies, but we're four and Winstanley is only one, and there is his son stranded in Africa with two broken legs. Could anything so dire happen to us, I ask myself. And I'm forced to reply—no, it couldn't. Do you think we might . . . ?"

"They're your silver coins, Calico," Jason said. "You must be the one to decide."

"No. I know you're captain, Jason, and all that, but I must

disagree with you. If we're Four for One and One for Four, as our motto says, then we must share and share alike."

"Very well, then," Jason said. "We'll take a vote." He felt for an instant a peculiar prickling sensation, a niggling tingle around the base of the Cap Of Deeper Thinking. He couldn't think what it might mean, so he went on, "Let's have a show of paws and wings. Those in favor of giving the Silver Reserve to Winstanley?"

All four voted *Yes*. Jason was glad that they had all been in agreement.

"Let's go back down right now," Oliver suggested, impatient as always, "and give it to him. I can't wait to see his face. I *told* him air travel was the thing."

Down they all trooped, with Calico holding the silver three-pennies. Winstanley was still sitting beside the fireplace. Behind the bar, Bertrand was washing up and polishing glasses. Everyone else had gone.

"You do the talking, Calico," Jason said. "Please."

So Calico did. She explained that they had all voted to give the Silver Reserve to Winstanley, and that they hoped it might enable him to reach Samuel more quickly. Winstanley looked overcome with surprise.

"Really, I don't know what to say. It's wonderfully kind of you. But I can't accept."

The next few minutes were taken up with Winstanley's repeated statement that, of course, he couldn't take the silver coins, and the four's repeated statement that, of course, he certainly could and would. Finally, Winstanley gave in.

"All right," he said. "I'll accept gratefully, for Samuel's sake. But we must regard the money as a loan. When I've got enough to repay you, I shall send a postal order. Will you give me your address, please?"

Bertrand produced paper and a pencil, and Calico printed. *Calico, Elm Cottage, Penn, Buckinghamshire, England.* Then, after many thanks from Winstanley, the four friends retired once more to the loft.

When they wakened and went down for breakfast, they found Winstanley had already gone.

"Couldn't wait, he couldn't," Bertrand chuckled. "Nothing would do but I should get him his evening tea early, so he could get a good night's start. *'I'm off into the wild blue yonder,'* he says to me, *'off by plane to Zanzibar and to the rescue.'* That excited, he was."

They were delighted to learn it, and soon they set off themselves, on their way to Londinium. The night was cool, and Jason was glad of Calico's warm fur which was rather like an eiderdown around him as they journeyed on, out of Stumbleton and along the winding road that led to the wide highway. Oliver was flying, scouting ahead, and Topaz was busily engaged in exploring every bramble bush and clump of bracken.

"When do we get to Londinium?" she kept asking. "Are we nearly there? How much longer to go, Calico?"

"It is surprisingly difficult to get any peace and quiet," Calico observed, "with *some* persons around. How on earth do I know how far we have to go, little T?"

Just then Oliver came flapping back. "Man on bicycle ahead," he announced.

There was the bicycle light and then there was the bicycle. On it rode a policeman and in a basket on the handlebars rode a large marmalade cat. As the constable whizzed past, the cat leaped out of the basket and landed beside Calico.

"Evening," he said politely. "I'm P. C. Wattles—Police Cat Wattles, that is. My mate, there, him on the bike, the human, he's just on his ordinary evening rounds, nothing special. But I'm on a case of my own, concerning our folk. I wonder if you could tell me, ma'am, if you've by any chance seen a handsome middle-aged cat, white and black, around here recently? He could be going under one of many names—he's got any number of 'em. Sometimes he calls himself Danielson, sometimes Flynte-Smythe, sometimes Winstanley . . ."

"Winstanley!" cried Jason, Oliver, Calico, and Topaz together. "Winstanley! Surely not. You can't mean *him?*"

"That's who I mean, right enough," P. C. Wattles said grimly. "I've been notified that he's in the area again and, if so, I intend to put an end to his little larks if I can. Him and his poor old mother who's stranded in Australia, or . . ."

"Or his son, Samuel," Jason put in, his heart quaking, "stranded in Zanzibar with two broken legs?"

"Yes, sir, that's another of his fancy dodges," P. C. Wattles said. "I take it, then, that you've encountered the gent?"

"Worse than that," Calico said in a sinking voice. "We've lent him all our money."

P. C. Wattles struck a paw against his forehead.

"Lent, ma'am?" he cried. "Lent? If you *will* lend money to the first stranger who gives you a sad convincing tale, then don't expect to see it ever again. I very much fear you've been conned."

"Conned?" Jason was remembering the tremor of doubt he had felt, and how he had dismissed it. Perhaps the Cap Of Deeper Thinking had been trying to warn him.

"Conned." P. C. Wattles repeated. "Swindled. Cheated.

Around these parts he's know as Stan the Con Cat. He's got more stories than you can shake a claw at, and they all sound genuine. I expect he offered you proof of his son's existence."

"Yes, indeed," Jason said. "He had a post card with a Zanzibar stamp on it. It looked very real."

"Naturally," P. C. Wattles said. "He always has something that looks like proof. If he's got a son in Zanzibar, then I'm a Siamese cat with pink-polka-dotted fur. Let's go back a bit now, and get the picture clear, shall we? How did you run into him?"

Jason explained.

"Aha," said P. C. Wattles. "Now, tell me this. Just before he came along and introduced himself, had you by any chance been discussing money?"

"Yes, we were!" Oliver recalled. "Don't you remember, Jason? Calico told us about the silver threepennies, and you said we'd call it the Silver Reserve."

"That's right," Jason said. "I do remember. Was he listening, do you think?"

"Of course!" Oliver cried. "He even *said* he'd been traveling in the field just beside the lane where we were. Oh, calamity! Woe and triple woe!"

Topaz began to cry. "What shall we do? What shall we do? Oh, I'm miserable!"

"Now, hang on a jiffy," P. C. Wattles said, writing in his note-book. "You didn't by any chance stay at an inn called The Danc-ing Monkey, did you?"

"The very place!" they all chorused.

"Hm, more and more interesting," P. C. Wattles said. "The innkeeper there is a jolly looking old cat bloke who calls himself Bertrand. In the force, we know him as Dirty Bertie. Very jovial, he is, very good host. But I suspect he's a sneaky character under it all. Can't ever prove anything, mind. That's the trouble. But we've had a notion for some time that he's working in league with Stan the Con Cat. Makes that inn his base of operations, as you might say. Stan lures the travelers there, and those whom he can't charm out of their wealth and possessions, Dirty Bertie robs in the night. You'd have lost those silver coins either way, mark my words."

Jason was really quite relieved to hear it. Even if they hadn't given the money to Winstanley, they might have wakened to find the coins gone. It seemed to make their decision less foolish, especially for Calico, who had made the suggestion in the first place. Jason did not want her to feel badly about it now.

He was sorry they had been sidetracked by Winstanley or that they had ever stopped at the inn and become so involved with the world of cats. True, Calico and Topaz had a right to their part in the quest, but it did not seem that the present situation would provide much opportunity for noble deeds. As for himself, Jason could not help feeling that time was passing and he was getting no nearer to his search, while his own molefolk at home continued in their desperate plight. *Patience, patience,* he told himself.

All this time Calico had said nothing. Absolute silence. But Jason, clinging to the reins around her neck, could feel her fur beginning to bristle. Her spine was curving alarmingly, and small electric sparks seemed to be coming from her dark fur. Calico was very, very angry. Suddenly, and without warning, she exploded.

"The viper!" she shrieked. "The heel! The lowdown good-for-nothing rat! The stinker! The snake-in-the-grass!"

P. C. Wattles looked distressed.

"Calm, calm, ma'am. I beg you."

"Calm!" shrilled Calico. "I'll give *him* calm! I'll knock him from here into the middle of next week!"

"Sh, Calico," Jason said. "P. C. Wattles is quite right. Raging won't do any good."

Oliver, who had been flying excitedly around in short swoops, now fluttered down beside Jason.

"If I may get a word in edgewise," he said hopefully, "I'd like to ask a question and make a modest sort of suggestion. Who

53

among us has wings? Answer—me, Oliver. Couldn't I do a sort of scouting-around trip? Couldn't I dash around hither and yon, and see if I can spot Winstanley?"

"Excellent idea," said P. C. Wattles. "Off you go, my lad, but first let *me* make a suggestion, if you don't mind. Try Stumbleton. Try the inn of The Dancing Monkey. Something tells me that Bert and Stan will be dividing the loot. Go on, now, and come back as quickly as you can."

"Ay, ay, sir!" caroled Oliver, saluting with a wingtip, quite carried away by his new role as detective.

Off he speedily flew, while the others settled themselves in a nearby thicket. They did not have long to wait. In less than half an hour, Oliver came panting in, making a neat landing beside Jason.

"Enemy sighted!" Oliver gasped. "Sure enough, he's back at The Dancing Monkey. I peered in without anyone noticing me, and guess what? Winstanley was chortling and saying to Bertrand: 'They're rather rare now, you know, the silver ones, so they may be worth a good deal.' Exactly what Calico said when she told us about the Silver Reserve. Open and shut case, if you ask me. Obviously he must have overheard us. Well, come on! Boot, saddle, to horse and away! Let's go! What are we waiting for? Onward!"

Oliver flew ahead, closely followed by Calico, who raced along in great bounding leaps like a panther, with Jason clinging tightly to the reins around her neck. Next came P. C. Wattles, puffing slightly, for he was rather stout. Topaz came last, rushing along as speedily as she could on her short young legs.

When they reached The Dancing Monkey they peeked carefully into the window of the cats' inn at the back of the old barn. The fire had died in the grate of the fireplace, and on the round oak table a single candle guttered low and spluttered with a bluish flame, causing two shadows to be thrown onto the wall, the shadows of the pair who were hunched around the table, huddled close together, talking in whispers. Bertrand and Winstanley.

Calico's wild fury had disappeared. Now she was calm. "With respect, Constable," she said to P. C. Wattles, "you stay here and let Captain Jason and myself go in."

"Well, I don't know about that." The police cat hesitated.

"Listen, Constable," Jason put in, "if you stay here, you can cover this way of escape."

"Very well, then," P. C. Wattles finally agreed.

"I want to come in, too, Cal, with you and Jason," Topaz insisted. "Oh, please let me. I'll be ever so helpful. I'll scratch like a lion. I'll groan like a ghost. They'll be terrified by me, I promise..."

"Hush," Oliver said sharply, grabbing her neck ribbon and

holding her so she could not rush to Calico's side. "If you don't keep your voice down, you'll ruin everything, you little moron."

"Oh Cal," Topaz wailed softly, "he's calling me names. Did you hear what he said? Tell him to stop it this minute . . ."

"Topaz, this is no time for quarrels," Jason said severely. "This is Calico's battle. You leave her alone."

Topaz sniffed a little, but was soon silent. Quietly, very quietly, Calico and Jason crept towards the door of the cats' inn. Quietly, very quietly, Jason stood on tiptoe and lifted the latch of the door handle. Quietly, very very quietly, Calico swung the door open with her paw. Then . . .

"Good evening, Winstanley," Calico said in a voice like thunder. "And how is your poor old mother, stranded in Australia? How do you plan to rescue your cousin from a raft in the middle of the North Atlantic ocean? What about your penniless sister in Siam? Are there any more?"

Bertrand's chubby body began to shake under his fur, and he sidled off rapidly behind the bar. Winstanley sprung to his feet with a ghastly look on his face.

"How did you get here?" he cried. "I mean, I don't know what you're talking about. Is something wrong?"

"You," snarled Calico, baring her teeth and showing her claws. "You. That's what's wrong. Come on, hand it over."

"Hand what over?" Winstanley whined. "Dear me, there must be some misunderstanding."

"Steady, Cal," Jason warned. "Don't lose your temper."

But it was no use. Calico had waited long enough. She sprang forward, with Jason hanging on desperately, afraid to let go and also afraid to find himself in the center of a cat fight.

"Misunderstanding!" Calico yowled. "There certainly was! We misunderstood you! Cockroach that you are! Louse! Earthworm! Hand over our silver or I'll tear you into tiny ribbons! Not for nothing was I known in my younger days as The Ferocious Lady. Gentle as I am towards my friends, to my enemies I'm the terror of ten counties!"

Calico's words had a strong effect upon Winstanley and Bertrand. They both took one horrified glance at her as she advanced upon them making hissing sounds deep in her throat. Then they both made a desperate scramble and leap, straight out the window, and straight into the waiting paws and claws of P. C. Wattles, Topaz, and Oliver.

"All right, me lad," roared the police cat, nabbing Winstanley. "We'll have the silver now, if you please."

"Gotcha!" yelled Topaz, pouncing upon the fleeing Bertrand.

"Hang on, little T!" Oliver cried. "I'll help you hold him.

Oh, good, Topaz! Two rousing cheers! One for you and one for me!"

"You're not such a bad old feather duster after all, Oliver," Topaz cried in return.

They were all talking at once and at the top of their voices; Winstanley and Bertrand denying everything, Calico saying, "Never mind all this nonsense, what about the Silver Reserve?" Oliver and Topaz telling each other how clever they both were, and Jason imploring everyone to be quiet.

Finally, in the midst of the uproar, P. C. Wattles tooted loudly on the police whistle which he carried on a thin brass chain around his neck. At the piercing sound, they all fell silent.

"Now then, ma'am," he addressed Calico, "I've searched Stan here, and Bert, and found your money, so here you are."

"It's thanks to you that we got it back," Calico said.

"All in a day's work," the police cat said with suitable modesty. "No need for you to stay any longer, now we've caught this pair. Where are you bound for?"

"Londinium," said Jason.

"Londinium?" P. C. Wattles said in surprise. "You must mean London, surely."

"Well, I don't know," Jason faltered. "It was called Londinium on the old map in Molanium, my native city . . ."

"Perhaps it used to be called that," the police cat said with a smile, "in the days of the Romans. But things have changed a bit since then. If you went waltzing into London these days, calling it Londinium, you'd get one or two odd glances, I wouldn't wonder. Look here. It's a good few miles away, so why not save your strength and go by truck? I've got a friend whose human is a long-distance truck driver. Great huge monstrous thing, that truck is, all loaded with fruits and vegetables for the London shops. They travel at night, mostly, and they get to Covent Garden—that's the big market—just at dawn. Suit you perfectly, that sort of trip. If you hurry, you can reach Molly's Cafe, on the main road, and catch them. Jenkins' human always pulls up there for a cup of tea. Just tell Jenkins that Wattles sent you and could he

59

please give you a lift. If you take this lane out of Stumbleton, turn left at the first crossroads and keep straight on until you reach the main road, you can't miss it."

They thanked the police cat and said good-by. When they were on their way, Calico grew thoughtful.

"You know what fooled me about Winstanley?" she said. "I thought he must be all right because he was a cat and so nicely mannered. We shall have to be extremely cautious in the future. *Extremely*. We will take no risks."

"No!" Jason blurted out in disagreement, surprising even himself. "In Molanium they were always saying *Be Cautious, Go Terribly Slow, Only Idiots Take Risks,* and all that sort of thing, but it seems to me that if you're going on a quest, risks are part of it. It isn't possible to take no risks at all, I mean, or you'd never be able to go anywhere."

"My, my," Oliver commented, "you *are* getting talkative, Jason, aren't you? Soon you'll be worse than I am. Natter, natter, natter. Don't take offense, you know I don't mean it. What should be our policy, then, in the future?"

Jason thought hard, touching the Cap Of Deeper Thinking for inspiration. "Reasonable care," he said at last. "We must just take reasonable care—and then bash on, regardless."

After some consideration, they all agreed upon this policy.
Topaz even tried to put it into a song:

Bash on, bash on in majesty,
And thwart the fouling churls—

"No use," she said at last. "Can't get any more lines. I just
have to take them as they come along, and I'm not even sure what
those first two lines mean."

"I thought they *sounded* quite impressive," said Jason, who
wasn't sure what they meant either. "Never mind. Let's sing our
motto song instead."

So as they walked along, they sang:

Four for One and One for Four,
Together till the journey's o'er.

Soon they had found their way to the main road, where the
cars with bright headlights swooped and plunged and snorted. Jason was stunned by the size and speed of the cars. They seemed
like enormous metal monsters, but then everything here in
Thither looked huge to him. Huge and fantastically fast moving.
How safe and small Molanium seemed now, and yet, strangely,
Jason did not want to return, not yet. There was an excitement

and the sense of possible adventure here which made him want to go on.

The friends made their way to Molly's Cafe, and there on one of the stools at the counter sat a broad-shouldered man in a heavy jacket and oil-stained trousers. At his feet sat a big gray cat with friendly amber eyes. Sure enough, the cat was none other than Jenkins.

"Glad to oblige," he said, when the four friends told him about P. C. Wattles. "Come with me, all you lot, and we'll get you stowed away before my guv'nor finishes his tea."

They scarcely had time to think about it before they found themselves snugly concealed between crates of cabbages and baskets of tomatoes.

"See you later," Jenkins winked.

Then he left them and in a moment the truck took off and they were speeding smoothly along the long road that led to London.

"I've been thinking," Jason said, pointing back towards Stumbleton. "Maybe the old map wasn't so wrong after all."

"What do you mean?" Oliver asked.

"*Here Be Dragons,*" Jason said with a smile. "That's what it said. And there were, in a way, weren't there?"

"That's right," Oliver agreed. "We've encountered our first peril. I wonder what the next will be?"

(3)

MRS. WEEPWORTHY
AND GLITTER LA FAY

All at once the truck came to a full stop. The four friends could hear the driver opening his door, climbing out, and slamming the door. Then they became aware of rattling sounds quite close to them.

"They're opening the back doors to unload the truck!" Calico whispered. "We've arrived! Quick, everyone—hide!"

Oliver was already nearly hidden by lettuce, so he simply burrowed down a little more deeply among the greenery. Jason dived headfirst in among some tomatoes, while Calico took refuge in a basket of cucumbers. Topaz, with her usual vanity, concealed herself under a pile of yellow lilies.

"I'm not sneaking in among the salad," she announced. "Flowers are more my style, don't you think?"

Jason found himself lifted high in his crate and swung out

of the truck and onto a vast stack of other crates. Sunlight poured into his eyes, blinding him, and for a few minutes he was too unnerved to do anything except huddle down among the round red tomatoes and shut his eyes tightly.

"I'll never be able to see a thing, not in this glare," he thought. "I'm blind and I've lost the others and I don't know what to do and I wish I were back home."

Then he remembered the sunglasses which Oliver had given him. He searched in his shoulder bag and found them. Once he had put them on, he discovered he could see quite well. Not perfectly, but enough to find his way around. This discovery heartened him a little, and he summoned the courage to peer over the top of the crate. One glance and he fell back dizzily and put his paws around a large tomato to steady himself.

His crate was the top one, and the pile was tremendously high in relation to the size of a mole. He wondered how he was ever going to get down to the ground.

"I shall break my neck if I try jumping," he told himself, "so that way is out. What else can I try?"

He decided to look around. The pile of tomato crates was like a tower, and from this vantage point Jason could see humans pushing full wide barrows; humans carrying sacks and boxes on their shoulders; humans buying and selling produce, and everywhere, everywhere fruit and vegetables and flowers, great stacks and mounds of them: cabbages, carrots, potatoes, Brussels sprouts, cauliflowers, onions, cucumbers, apples, raspberries, strawberries, plums, roses, and gladioli. The name Jenkins had mentioned now came back to Jason. *Covent Garden.*

"My first day in London," thought Jason, a little bitterly, "and here I am lost among the lettuce, bamboozled by bushels of beans, and trapped in a tower of tomatoes."

Then a very frightening thought struck him. All these crates and baskets of garden produce were being bought by merchants and shopkeepers and were being carted away to sell in shops all over London. If he, Jason, small and almost paralyzed with fear as he was, did not get out immediately, he might be separated from his friends forever.

Necessity gave him daring. Without losing any more time, he drew out the spool of thread which his mother had packed for him. Tying an end firmly to one of the slats of the tomato crate, he shoved the spool over the edge and let it fall. It landed on the ground without any of the bustling humans having noticed it. Jason hoped the thread would bear his weight. Carefully he climbed over the edge of the box. Grasping the thread tightly between his paws, he began to lower himself down.

Zing! Faster and faster he slid down on the thread, until—plop! There he was on the ground, imprisoned in his tower no longer. Now all he had to do was find the others. With his sunglasses wedged firmly onto his nose, his bag slung over one shoulder, and his mauve and green striped cap on his head, Jason set off.

The human crowd was large, tightly packed and noisy. Jason, scurrying from one mountain of vegetables to another, was afraid that one of the giant human boots would accidentally step on him and squash him. He darted between the hurrying boots, skipping this way and that to avoid them. Then, from just ahead, came the most welcome sound Jason had ever heard.

"Jason! Thank goodness!"

With one leap, Calico was beside him. Gratefully, Jason climbed on her back.

"Safe at last from all those huge human feet," he gasped. "Whew! I thought I'd never find you. Where are the others?"

"Topaz is waiting over there, beside those flowers," Calico said, "and Oliver is scouting around, looking for you. We've been terribly worried, and you know what Oliver is like. So excitable. He's probably miles away by now, never stopping to think that you couldn't possibly have gone far, as you can't see much in daylight."

"Oh, the sunglasses work pretty well," Jason said. "I can get along."

Swoop! There was Oliver, beside them. "Delighted to hear it," he cried. "And delighted to see you again, Jason. My sunglasses work pretty well, too. Of course, owls don't have quite such difficulty in sunlight as moles do, but still, without Gran's glasses, my vision would be seriously impaired. Badly distorted, one might say. In other words, just plain awful. Good old Gran. London's wonderful, isn't it? Everything whirling along, terrific action, lots of excitement on all sides. Oh, I nearly forgot. I should've said, chief of signals reporting for duty, captain!"

"Hello, Oliver," Jason said, hanging onto Calico's fur in order to prevent himself being bowled over by the affectionate slap on the back from Oliver's strong wings. "Yes, it's very exciting, but I've been wondering . . ."

"Wondering what?" Oliver inquired.

"Well," Jason said thoughtfully, "now that we're actually here in London, where do we go? How do we begin the search?"

"That's for you to figure out," Oliver said easily and confidently. "You're captain. And you're ever so clever, Jason. Think of all that ancient history you told me when I visited Molanium."

It was all very well for Oliver to have faith in him, thought Jason. But it wasn't so easy for a relatively inexperienced mole to venture into Thither at all, much less into this gigantic human city. As for deciding how to begin the quest for a cure to rid Molanium of the invisible sickness, Jason somehow felt that a knowledge of ancient history wasn't quite enough. He wondered if he would ever get used to the vastness and confusion of things here in Thither. The inn of The Dancing Monkey had seemed very large and noisy at the time, but it was quiet and tiny compared to London. He touched the Cap Of Deeper Thinking for reassurance. Maybe he would discover what to do and where to go. He hoped so.

"Goodness, you've been gone a long time," Topaz said. "And where were *you*, Jason? Calico and Oliver were frantic with worry. I knew you'd turn up, but did they listen to me? Oh, no. Worry, worry, worry. I don't believe in worrying. It makes wrinkles on the brow, and my brows are really quite attractive. It would be a pity to spoil them. Pretty rhymes with pity; could it be a verse?"

"Hush, Topaz," Calico said, "and let's make plans."

Just then, they all heard shrill titters of laughter. Mocking laughter. Scornful laughter. Unpleasant laughter. Glancing around, they saw two sleek mice swaggering towards them. The mice were large, as mice go, and they wore high black leather boots and wide black leather belts with large buckles of silver shaped to form the letter B.

"What have we here, Charlie?" one mouse said to the other.

"A little party of tourists, I believe," the second mouse said. "Up from the country for the day. Bus tours and all that. Iced buns for tea. Well, well, well. Think we ought to show 'em around, Jacko?"

"Hardly worth the bother, I'd say," the mouse called Jacko replied.

Calico's fur started faintly bristling. "All right, young mice," she said in a severe dignified voice. "That's enough out of you. I don't like your tone of voice, and I don't like mice being rude to me, either."

"Simmer down, Ma," Charlie said. "You might meet a spot of trouble if you're not careful."

"Why, you cheeky little . . ." Calico began.

Then, as Jason tugged with all his strength on her neck reins, she stopped short.

"You're right, my dear," she said to him. "Mustn't get annoyed over nothing. That's no way to begin."

Charlie dug an elbow into Jacko's ribs, and both hooted with derisive laughter.

"Nothing!" Charlie wheezed. "Did you hear what the poor old dear said, Jacko? She called us Nothing!"

"I heard, I heard, Charlie. Think the G.R. would like to hear?"

"Who or what," demanded Calico, "is the G.R.?"

The two mice smiled, sly, secretive sinister smiles. "You'll find out," they said.

Then they vanished into the forest of trampling human boots.

"I didn't like them," Topaz said. "They gave me the shivers."

Jason agreed. "I think we should get out of here," he said. "I didn't like the looks of them at all. Did you notice they were both carrying knives in their belts? I think we should depart with all possible speed."

"Good idea," Calico said. "Heavens! I wonder if all the London mice are like those two?"

"Certainly not," said a mouse voice nearby. "Those two are up to no good, and I would advise you to keep well away from them. But please don't judge all mice by them."

They turned, and there under a flower stall was a short and stubby brown mouse who had a small stall of his own. He, however, was not selling flowers but newspapers.

"Just arrived, have you?" he asked. "Thought so. Care for

the morning papers? *Daily Mousegraph. The Canine Times. Catchester Guardian. The Pigeon Post.* All the latest news."

"No, thanks," Jason said. "We aren't very, that is, we haven't much money."

The newsstand mouse laughed heartily. "Not necessary. Pay in seeds or whatever you happen to have. Wouldn't have a bit of cheese would you? Here. This is an absolute essential if you're going to see London. *The Smaller Edition Of The London A to Z.* It's put out especially for our sort of folk, but in all respects the same as the larger or human edition. All the streets of London, neatly listed and mapped. See?"

They looked, and decided the book was a necessity.

"Would you take a gooseberry cake for it?" Jason asked, fishing in his bag.

"Would I?" the newsstand mouse squeaked happily. "I should say I would. Haven't tasted a gooseberry cake since I was a youngster in the country. There you are, and the best of luck to you."

"By the way," Jason said, "what did those two mice mean by G.R.? And why were their belt buckles in the shape of a B?"

The newsstand mouse turned pale and glanced around nervously. "The less said, the better. Don't know anything about it, I don't. Safer that way."

Jason could see that they were not going to learn anything further here. Perhaps the mystery would be cleared up later. So, saying good-by to the newsstand mouse, they set off to explore the city.

Streets and streets and streets. The huge feet of all manner of hurrying humans. The honking and whizzing and roaring of cars and taxi cabs. Doorways and steps, windows and shops, enormous signs and billboards, restaurants and cafes, theaters. The four friends began to get very tired. It was midmorning, after all, and long past their sleeping time.

"I'm exhausted," Topaz complained. "Can't we find some place to get a decent day's sleep, Jason, and then do some more exploring tonight?"

"Yes, I think we must," Jason agreed. "What's this place we're coming to? It looks likely. It looks *safe*."

The sign was in white letters on a blue background, with a red circle behind.

"*Underground*," Jason read aloud, with a tone of longing in his voice. "It does sound appealing, doesn't it? Shall we go in and see?"

How different London was from Molanium. The sign gave Jason a twinge of homesickness, and for a moment he longed to be back again with his mother and his sisters in their snug underground house.

"It says something else," Calico said, peering hard. "*Leicester Square*. I wonder what that means?"

Oliver was riffling one wingtip hastily through the London A to Z. As chief of signals, he felt it his duty to do the map-reading and establish their whereabouts.

"Got it!" he cried. "That's the street where we are. Not that it helps much. I mean, this is Leicester Square up here, but what's down there, underground? I don't think I share your feelings about going down, Jason. Quite natural for a mole—I realize that. But as an owl, and therefore as a member of the birdfolk, I tend to feel a little, well, *trapped* when I'm not in the open air."

"Oh, dear," Jason said heavily. "Yes, I do see that, Oliver. What shall we do, though? We can't possibly sleep out here on the street, with all this noise and confusion and daylight."

He could feel himself growing sadder and sadder. His longing for a resting place in some safe underground burrow almost overwhelmed him, and yet he did not want to be unfair to Oliver.

"It's all right," Oliver said staunchly. "You go on down, and

73

I'll fly around here and find a nook somewhere. There's bound to be a quiet corner up high—a window ledge, perhaps. We'll meet this evening at dusk at this same spot, right under the sign."

"Are you sure, Oliver?" Jason asked anxiously.

"Quite sure," Oliver said. "Don't worry. I shall be quite all right."

"It's only that I hate us to get separated," Jason said. "Just in case. But I expect you're right. Until this evening, then."

Oliver flew off and Calico, Jason and Topaz proceeded through the wide doorway.

Bustle and din met their eyes and ears once more. The place seemed to be overflowing with humans, rushing this way and that. The two cats, with Jason clinging to Calico's neck fur, slipped through the crowds and before they knew it, they found themselves on a staircase. It was a very different kind of staircase from anything they had ever seen, for it was moving. Moving, in a clanking way, steadily downward.

"Where are we going?" Topaz wailed. "Cal, I'm scared! We're going down into the middle of the earth. Maybe as far as the other side, even. I don't want to go to Australia!"

"Hush," Calico said sharply. "We're not on the way to Australia, silly. I'm not quite sure where we *are* going, exactly, but we'll soon find out."

"I think," Jason said in an awed voice, "that this is part of

74

some huge underground city. Like Molanium, you know, only much, much bigger."

He began to wonder if perhaps there might be a race of giant moles who had built these mighty tunnels and caverns. What would they be like? How would they feel about a modestly sized mole such as himself? He began to compose a short speech for use in approaching a giant mole. *Venerable Sir,* he would say, *I bring you greetings from the molefolk of Molanium, a mole city whose history goes back in an honorable and unbroken line to Roman times.* Perhaps the answer to his quest lay right here. Perhaps the giant moles would be both kindly and wise. Perhaps they would be able to tell him what ailed Molanium and how to defeat the invisible sickness. Jason's heart began to beat more quickly.

At the bottom of the moving staircase, they found themselves faced with an assortment of high vaulted tunnels. Choosing one, they dashed along, avoiding the numerous humans who were cluttering up the place. Jason was astonished at the presence of humans. Was it possible that they and the giant moles shared this underground city?

Finally they emerged onto a platform, and when they came to the edge of it, they saw shiny, silver-colored rails running in a straight line.

"Why, it's a railway!" Topaz exclaimed. "An underground railway! Whee! Shall we have a ride? Where's the train?"

Jason felt terribly disappointed. There were no giant moles after all. This underground place belonged to humans.

"I think," Calico said in a low warning voice, "that we're in immediate danger. See that man in the uniform, with the word *Guard* on his cap? He's seen us, and he has a very grim look on his face. Quick, my dears, down from the platform. He won't follow us there."

The guard strode purposefully towards them, but before he could reach them, Topaz and Calico had jumped down onto the space beside the tracks.

"Hey! Stop those cats!" the guard shouted.

Too late. The platform was filled with surging people and the cats had disappeared.

"That's odd," the guard said. "Could've sworn I saw two cats here. Well, if they get near the tracks, they'll be done for, that's certain."

His loud voice echoed faintly down to Jason and the cats. They looked at one another in dismay.

"Stay well away from the tracks, little T," Calico muttered. "Come on, squeeze over as close to the platform as you can. Now, don't worry. It's going to be all right."

Just then they heard the train. Swifter than wind, louder than cannons, the train came tearing along the silvery tracks. Each split-second brought it nearer and nearer to the three friends cowering beside the tracks. *Was the quest to end this way? Had they come this far, only to be run over by an underground train?*

Jason had thought he was prepared for adventures, but he had not bargained for this kind of peril. His instinct told him to scamper, to find a hole somewhere and dig himself into it. But how could he leave the cats? He must at least try to act like captain, although at the moment he felt only like a defenseless and absolutely terrified mole, quite out of his element.

"Flatten yourselves against the side as much as you can," Jason heard himself say in a surprisingly calm voice. "That way, it may just possibly miss us."

Faster and nearer came the train. More quickly and fearfully beat the hearts of the three. Jason had a sudden awful thought: if anything happened to them, Oliver would never know. How long would he hover around the Underground sign, waiting for the friends who would never appear again? A slight dampness came to Jason's eyes, and he blinked. Beside him, Topaz sobbed quietly.

The train was almost upon them. Then, all at once, just behind them, a small unsuspected door opened and a pair of thin black paws reached out.

"Well, I suppose you'd better come in," the voice said, "although goodness knows I can't abide cats. Bear witness, oh ye Heavens! I am sacrificing my very safety for the sake of this mole lad."

They had no time to question or even to look. In they darted, to safety, just as the electric underground train hurtled alongside the exact place where they had been crouching.

"Talk about narrow escapes!" Calico breathed. "I swear my fur must've turned gray with fright."

They looked around them, and saw that they were in a neatly kept dwelling place directly under the platform. Lace curtains adorned the one window. The sitting room was furnished with a sofa made out of a matchbox and upholstered in deep purple velvet, a table with a gold-tasseled crimson velvet cloth, and several armchairs covered with velvet of delphinium blue.

In front of them stood their rescuer, a stooped and wizened mole lady of advancing years, clad in a long rustling silk dress of robin-breast red. Around her neck she wore a wafting white ostrich feather boa, and on her head a pastel blue frilled duster cap.

Jason jumped down from Calico's back and swept as low and gracious a bow as he could manage. "Madam, we cannot thank you enough," he said. "To whom do we owe our lives?"

The mole lady reached out a fragile paw and touched Jason's shoulder. "My, my, proper manners you've got, I see," she said. "I'm Mrs. Weepworthy. Late of the London stage. London and Brighton, actually. *Glitter La Fay,* that was my stage name in the good old days when I was with the M and M—the Mouse and Mole Troupers, that was, and a finer and pluckier group of entertainers you never did see. *The show must go on!* The cry of the true trouper, and go on it did, for lo! those many years. Through shine and, more frequently, rain. Ah, past glories! Ah, fame! Ah, names in lights! Ah, the stomp of the audience's feet! Ah, the wild clapping of paws! Ah, me!"

Calico and Topaz looked at each other questioningly. Never in their lives had they encountered anyone like this. Jason, too, was slightly taken aback, but as the old lady was a member of the molefolk and had saved their lives, he felt he must be careful to be courteous and not to offend her.

"We are honored, ma'am," he said, trying to speak formally, for he felt this was expected of him. "How is it that you live here now, if I may ask?"

Mrs. Weepworthy struck a tragic pose, one paw to her eyes. "Time," she said in a sorrowful voice. "Time passes, young mole. The years fly away on raven wing and all things change. Glitter La Fay is no more. Now I am plain Mrs. Weepworthy. Have been for ages, to tell you the truth. Widowed these many years. I like to live here in the Leicester Square Underground because the old *Mousedrome* used to be near here. In the cellars of the larger but certainly no more famous or better *Hippodrome*. Ah, that was the place, the old Mousedrome! The tales I could tell! In its heyday, it had the greatest performers in the entire Smaller Animals' Society. That was real music hall, that was, not like you get now with that young Perdita or whatever her name is, doing those daft dances they all seem to like these days. Ah, memories, memories!"

Mrs. Weepworthy began to weep softly, while Jason and the cats looked on in embarrassment, not knowing what to say. At last she took a corner of her ostrich feather boa and wiped her eyes.

"Well, come along now," she said in a different and quite cheery voice. "Expect you'd like your tea, wouldn't you? Then a bit of a rest. Let's see what we've got; two or three pieces of shortbread and some chocolate. Surprising how much chocolate I collect from the platform. Humans are awfully wasteful. Always throwing bits carelessly away. I don't live badly at all, here. By the way, you haven't told me your names, and whether or not these cats are *reliable,* if you see what I mean."

"I'm Jason," said Jason, "and this is Calico and Topaz, and yes, they're very reliable."

"Any friend of Jason's is a friend of ours," Calico said loyally. "And we're all extremely grateful to you, Mrs. Weepworthy, for saving us from that train."

"Brr—when I think of it . . ." Topaz shuddered.

Mrs. Weepworthy began skipping around nimbly, preparing the tea. Despite her age, she was very agile.

"I don't expect you'd have actually been hurt," she said, "but I thought I'd best not take the chance. I did dither a bit before I decided to invite you in. Cats, I mean. No offence, but the Mousedrome was greatly troubled by the Hippodrome's stage cat. A proper old Tartar, he was. Many's the time I've gone through a performance with one eye on the door in case old Satan appeared. I suppose your nerves were frazzled just now, wondering if your last hour had come. Well, never mind. Nothing like a little drama to add spice to life, I always say."

Mrs. Weepworthy, Jason decided, had two voices—her ordinary voice and her theatrical voice.

"Were you an actress, ma'am?" he asked.

Mrs. Weepworthy paused in mid-skip, with the teapot in her paws. Jason could almost see her stage self coming on again. Sure enough, the busily tea-preparing Mrs. Weepworthy became once more Glitter La Fay, late of the London and Brighton stage.

"Ah, no, my pet," she sighed. "An actress I was not. No, that was not my fate. Glitter La Fay was not born to play high tragedy. I was gifted with another gift." She paused, threw back her head a little, and waved the teapot in a graceful gesture. "Mine," she said, "was a golden voice."

"Coo!" Topaz whispered. "Do you think we shall ever get our tea, Cal?"

"Sh!" Calico hissed commandingly. "I'm rather taken by her. You're too young to appreciate her, little T."

"You *will* misunderstand me, won't you?" Topaz said, in an injured voice. "I think she's super, but I'm starving."

81

Jason, meantime, had decided what he must say. He hoped he would get the speech right.

"D-dare we hope, Mrs. Weepworthy," he stammered, "that you might favor us with a song?"

"Good old captain," murmured Topaz. "There goes our tea, while she does her canary bit."

Mrs. Weepworthy set the teapot down on the crimson velvet tablecloth. Her face was all smiles, faintly faraway and prepared to be sorrowful, but still eager.

"If you would really care to hear one short rendition . . ."

"Oh, yes!" they all chorused politely. "Please do!"

Mrs. Weepworthy swept regally to the middle of the sitting room floor, ignoring the *z-z-z-zim!* of the underground train that had just come to a halt outside her door. She rearranged her feather boa around her neck, patted her blue duster cap, and took up her singing position, paws lightly clasped in front of her, back very straight so as to be able to breathe deeply.

Then she began to sing. Her voice, although no longer as strong as it once might have been, was true and clear. As she sang, she made various gestures, rolling her eyes heavenwards, flinging out one paw to emphasize the words she was trilling. Here is the song she sang:

(T U N E : *She's Only a Bird in a Gilded Cage*)

She was only a mole maid on Hampstead Heath,

And he was a dashing mole lad.

You might think of their love as a flower wreath,

But alas, it was terribly sad.

For he wanted to wander the wide world o'er,

Sail into the storm's wild teeth,

So off he did roam,

While she stayed at home,

Lonely mole maid of Hampstead Heath.

On the last notes, Mrs. Weepworthy rose to her tiptoes, then sank, swirled, and bowed to her audience.

Jason clapped like fury and gave one or two rousing cheers.

"Bravo!" shouted Topaz. "Hurrah, hurrah for Glitter La Fay! That's a verse."

"A lovely song," declared Calico. "Very touching. Very."

Mrs. Weepworthy was now truly transformed. "Ah, my friends!" she cried, kissing her pawtips and blowing kisses towards Jason and the cats. "Glitter La Fay was a singer of many tunes. Yes, indeed, my lovelies, I can truthfully assure you that in those oft-remembered days, no troupers worth their salt could do only one turn. By no means. You could bet your last penny on that. Not only could I sing tragical pieces like the one I have just rendered for your entertainment and enlightenment. I could also do comical songs. This one, now, used to knock 'em in the aisles."

With that, Mrs. Weepworthy flung off her duster cap, nipped smartly over to a cupboard, drew out an old top hat, rammed it on

her head at a rakish angle, hitched up her long rusty silk skirts a notch, revealing black buttoned boots, snatched up the straight pin which served as a fire poker, twirled it like a cane, and sang with a cockney accent this song:

(T U N E : *The Old Kent Road*)

Last night down our alley came a rat,
A sly old geezer looking dreadful fat.
Sees our 'Arry, then 'e tips 'is 'at,
In a slightly mocking kind of way.
          Oh!
"Now, young mouse, and is your mother near?
  Tell 'er that the rent collector's 'ere."
"Right-o, Guv'nor," answers 'Arry clear,
  Like as if 'is mother meant to pay.
          Oh!
"Wot cheer!" 'Arry calls to me.
" 'E's no rent collector,
  'E's no 'ouse inspector."
Well, now, wot you make of that?
We whistled for the old alley cat
          (Oh, what a dust-up!)
We whistled for the old alley ca-a-t!

By this time, they were all cheering enthusiastically. Jason clapped until his paws were sore. Calico cried *More!* Even Topaz had stopped thinking about her hunger and was in a good mood.

85

Then Mrs. Weepworthy took off the top hat and replaced her duster cap on her head.

"Well, well, well," she said. "Happy bygone days. Let's have some tea, and maybe later I'll show you my scrapbook. You'd hardly believe the nice things the newspapers said about me once. *Darling Of The Mousedrome Triumphs Again. Glitter Glitters Anew In Last Night's Performance.* Etcetera, etcetera. Still, you do need to get some sleep. I can see that you're drooping, Jason, and your cat friends, too. I mustn't bore you."

"No, no," Jason protested earnestly. "It's been wonderful, Mrs. Weepworthy—er—Madame La Fay."

"You're quite the nicest young mole I've met in many a long day," the ex-singer said. "Now, tea and sleep all of you."

When the evening came, they all wakened refreshed, to find Mrs. Weepworthy waiting with a fresh pot of tea.

"I don't suppose," she said wistfully, "you'd care to stay awhile? A year or so? We could all get on so well, I'm certain."

"I'm sorry," Jason said, "but I'm afraid we couldn't stay." He explained about the quest and about the invisible sickness which was destroying the ancient mole city.

"Would you happen to know where we might find some wise mole doctor, Mrs. Weepworthy?" he asked. "Or would you, perhaps, have any ideas on the subject yourself? Any remedies which might work?"

"I fear not," she replied. "Singing was my profession, Jason, not nursing or doctoring."

"In that case," Jason said regretfully, "we really must be on our way."

Mrs. Weepworthy heaved a deep sigh and looked dramatic again. "I didn't suppose you really would stay," she said. "Ah, life! Ah, fate! Ah, withered rosebuds! Ah, the old Mousedrome, long faded. Ah, me, long faded. Alas! A long alas!"

They all felt dreadful. Jason looked away, not daring to look at the others in case he gave way to tears. Topaz was sniffing openly. Even Calico had to try very hard to maintain her usual appearance of calm.

Mrs. Weepworthy looked at them all, and then she smiled. "Oh, come now," she said in her un-stage voice. "You don't want to take an old trouper all that seriously. Nothing like a bit of drama, I always say, so perhaps I do lay it on a bit thick from time to time. Don't worry about me, my pets. I shall get on fine. I have so far, haven't I? If you ever pass this way again, I'd be delighted to see you."

"We'll try," Jason said, from the depths of his heart. "And we'll never forget you."

"Take this," Mrs. Weepworthy said. "It's my card. I don't

need them any more, of course, but it's one of the ones I used to use in the old days. It'll remind you of me, and who knows? It might come in useful sometime—my name, you know, if ever you happen to meet anyone who knew me at the height of my fame."

Jason took the card gently, and read it:

GLITTER LA FAY
Singer · *Chanteuse* · *Comedienne*
LONDON AND BRIGHTON
STAGE.
Velvet Cottage, Track Side, Leicester Square,
London. W.C.2.

"Thank you," he said. He wished he knew what else to say. If only they could stay, to keep Mrs. Weepworthy company. But it was impossible. He climbed on Calico's back, and the three of them said good-by. Mrs. Weepworthy gave them a few squares of chocolate to sustain them in case of sudden hunger.

"Just remember one thing, Jason," she said.

"What's that?" he asked.

"The show must go on," Mrs. Weepworthy said. "Even when you're discouraged. Even when the prompter starts sneezing and the piano player faints and the audience is asking for its money back. The show must go on. Remember."

Jason could not imagine himself having this kind of endurance, but he did not want to hurt the old mole lady's feelings. "I—I . . ." he stammered. "Well, I'll *try* to try."

"Who could say more?" Mrs. Weepworthy said. "Mind the step as you go out, won't you? And be sure to dash up onto the platform quickly, in between trains. Cheerios, my dearios!"

Then they were out, and onto the platform, and away into the great tunnels, and the moving staircase was carrying them up, up, up towards the London evening, where Oliver would be waiting.

(4)

NICOLETTE AND

THE PERSIAN ROOM

Outside Leicester Square underground station, the evening was gray and mild. The streets were filled with humans, in a hurry as they always seemed to be, and the neon signs were winking and blinking in blues and reds and yellows. A sprinkling of late sparrow flurried past on their way home. But there was no sign of Oliver.

"This really is stupid of him," Calico said. "Now we shall have to sit here, waiting, while he's flying all over London, seeing the sights."

"He's always accusing other people of being late," Topaz put in, "but when it comes to him, it's a different matter."

"I hope," Jason said in a worried voice, "that nothing has happened to him."

Topaz and Calico glanced at Jason in alarm.

"What could've happened to him?" Calico asked. "He's got wings. He can easily escape from any danger."

"I don't know," Jason replied unhappily. "It's just that I've got a strange prickling sensation under the rim of the Cap Of Deeper Thinking. And several times before, when I felt that way, it meant, well, it seemed rather like a warning, when I thought of it later, because something perilous *did* happen."

Topaz began to wail. "Oh, Oliver! Something awful has happened. I just know it! And yesterday, when we were going around all those streets, and Oliver was riding on my back, and I was tired, I told him I wished he'd get lost. But I didn't mean it. Truly, I didn't. I didn't, did I, Calico?"

"Of course you didn't, my dear," Calico said reassuringly. "And anyway, that wouldn't make it happen. Don't upset yourself needlessly."

"We must look carefully," Jason said, thinking hard. "We must first search the immediate area."

They began poking into every possible corner of the entrance to the underground station. Topaz ran around in circles, calling, "Oliver! Where are you? SOS! Save Oliver's Soul! Help!"

Finally Calico told her to hush or they'd attract attention from the humans, and goodness knows what might happen.

They looked in the street. They looked up at window ledges. They stared into the air. But Oliver was nowhere to be seen. Jason was beginning to get really panicky. He could not think what to do next. Then, just as he was trying to work out a plan, Calico gave a shout. "Look! Up there!"

"Is it Oliver?" asked Jason, his heart bounding with hope.

But it was not Oliver. It was a sparrow, winging towards them. This, in itself, would not have been surprising, except for one thing. In his beak, the sparrow was carrying a red and white spotted handkerchief.

"Beauty's flag!" cried Jason. "It's a signal from Oliver! Oh, I knew, I just *knew* he would need it sometime to signal distress."

The sparrow landed with a flourish of his short wings and laid the handkerchief in Jason's paws.

"Guess you're the bloke I'm after," he chirped. "Just about played out, I am, after that hop. I've never flown so fast in my life. Your friend's in bad trouble, mate. He sent this flag or whatever it is, so you'd believe me. Bad trouble, that's what he's in."

"What's happened to him?" they all demanded at once.

"Got himself in a right mess, he has," the sparrow went on. "He's in a cage over on Bond Street. Cage in a boutique window."

"Boo-*teek?*" Topaz said, bewildered. "What's that?"

"Well, there's boutiques and boutiques," the sparrow said, "but this one's a posh shop. Sells jewelry and handbags and a few dresses, all very expensive. The sort of place the ladies don't ask how much a thing costs—they just say *I'll have six of those, please.*"

"Heavens!" gasped Calico. "Don't tell me they're going to sell Oliver!"

"Oh, no," laughed the sparrow. "He's just there for window decoration. Behind bars, old Oliver is. *Tell them,* he begs me, *tell them to come and rescue me.* Slipped the flag to me, he did, and managed to gasp a message before they took him inside the shop, him being held in a shopping bag at the time, yelling for help, and me hearing and darting down to see what was going on. It's amazing the humans didn't notice, but they're not very sharp-eyed. So here I am."

"How do we get there?" Jason inquired, for he had just remembered that their book of London street maps was with Oliver.

"Simple! Just follow me," said the sparrow.

They were off. The sparrow flew in short spurts, waiting on every street corner for the three to catch up. Along pavements they sped, across roads, under taxicabs, and through what seemed like a wild stampede of human feet.

At last they came to a street where most of the shops were small but expensive looking. The sparrow stopped and pointed. "There you are," he said. "Feast your eyes."

The name of the shop was *Nicolette,* painted in flowing gold letters on a white background. By standing on their hind legs, Topaz and Calico could see into the shop window. Jason, clutching Calico's neckreins, had a very good view. And what a terrifying sight it was.

The shop window itself contained an attractive display: several scarves of fine white silk, a gold bracelet and necklace, an elegant white dress, a small gold-colored evening bag. Everything was either white or gold, and there were no price tags on anything. At one side of the window there was a high wicker stand, painted white. Suspended from the stand was a brass bird cage, polished until it looked almost like gold. In the bird cage was Oliver.

Patience was not one of Oliver's more noticeable qualities. Nor was he one to accept his fate meekly. He was at this moment furiously agitated. He shook the bars of his cage with his wingtips. He paced. He jumped up and down in rage. And more than anything, he protested loudly. The few passing humans on the street took his cries of *Whoo-whoo-whoo* for normal owl noises, and said how charming he was. But his three friends could hear his voice plainly through the plate-glass window and could understand his words.

"Oh, the shame of it!" Oliver was ranting. "The disgrace! The everlasting awfulness! To be caught just like that by a fiendish human lady when I was minding my own business, sitting peacefully on the pavement in the sunshine in Leicester Square.

The insult of it! I'll never forget what she said. 'A tiny tawny owl,' she said. 'How sweet,' she said. 'How adorably different it'd look in the shop window,' she said. 'Too marvelous,' she said. And all the time I sat there, blinking like the idiotic owl I am, not realizing what she intended. Popped a straw shopping bag over me, she did. How dare she? Whatever will my Gran say, if she ever gets to hear of it? I'll never live it down! Oh, the pity of it! Why didn't I fly up to a window ledge or a roof, instead of sitting there on the pavement? Why didn't I take off the moment I heard somebody speaking about me? I never thought anyone would actually capture an owl, that's why. Betrayed by my trustful nature, that's me. I'm done for! Help! Let me out! Will no one hear the appeals of an unlawfully imprisoned owl? Help, I say!"

Jason tapped softly on the heavy plate glass. But Oliver was making so much commotion that it was a moment or so before Jason could attract his attention, and all the time Jason was quivering with nervousness, wondering what would happen if any human passers-by happened to notice two cats and a mole attempting to communicate with the owl in Nicolette's window.

At last Oliver glanced down. "Jason!" he breathed. "You've come! Oh, thank goodness. Please get me out quickly."

But how? Jason wondered. It was evening, so the shop was closed. They could not slip in through the door. But if they waited until morning, they would never be able to carry out a rescue, for the shop would be full of humans. No, it would have to be done at night. Getting inside the shop wasn't going to be easy, though. And even if they did manage to get in, it would not be easy to free Oliver, for the shop window was lighted with several brilliant spotlights.

"This is going to be tricky," Jason murmured.

They noticed, then, that the sparrow was still with them and was sitting on the shop doorstep looking mildly amused.

"The back way," he said. "It's the only thing."

"Pardon?" Jason said, not understanding.

"The back way into the shop," the sparrow repeated. "Go around the block, turn into the alley and find the back entrance. You cats won't be able to get in, more than likely, but this young fellow will. Must be a crack somewhere. Here, come on. I'll show you."

They followed the sparrow as he sped past people and shops along the pavement, until they came to a turning. Then more turnings, until at last they found themselves in an alley full of back doors and dust bins.

"Here," the sparrow puffed, pointing a wingtip. "There's the back entrance to Nicolette's. Now, mates, I'll be leaving you. My old lady will have had the tea ready for ages, and she'll be mad as blazes if I don't get home soon."

With that, he flew off before they could thank him for all his kindness. Then they began to examine the back door and the windows of Nicolette's. Jason's eye lit on something hopeful: a small piece of paper stuck into one corner of the window. Quickly, he climbed the drainpipe, reached the window ledge, poked at the paper with his paw and, sure enough, there was a hole in the window pane underneath and the paper had been used to cover it.

"Well, well," he said to the cats. "The shop's not quite so high class at the back as it is at the front, and lucky for us, too. I can just squeeze in, but goodness knows how Oliver will be able to get out."

"Make the hole larger," Calico suggested. "All you need to do is break the glass a little, with a sharp implement such as a pair of scissors. Must be something like that inside there. Mind you don't break the whole thing, though, or we'll be certain to be heard."

"Right-o," Jason said, feeling a tremendous sense of adventure. "Here I go. Wish me luck."

Just then they heard a loud voice. It was a cat voice, and it was singing. Furthermore, it was coming closer and closer. The words of the song were enough to make the three friends stare at one another in dismay.

Thieves and robbers had better scat,
Here comes the mighty nightwatch cat!

97

"What shall we do?" Jason cried in an alarmed whisper. "He's sure to think we're trying to break in."

"We *are* trying to break in," Topaz pointed out, reasonably enough.

"Hush, silly," Calico said. "Jason means the nightwatch cat will think we're trying to steal something."

"Well, we're trying to steal Oliver, aren't we?" Topaz insisted.

"Why did we ever bring *you* along?" Calico said. "You and your arguments at the worst possible moments."

"Well, I wish I'd never come along," Topaz retorted. "No one cares sixpence about me."

"I'm going to slip in quickly," Jason decided. "You two try to get rid of the watch cat, and try not to let him notice that the paper's been torn away from the window. It's our only hope. Do your best!"

With that, he slid in through the hole in the window and disappeared. For once, Calico was flustered.

"We're lost!" she moaned. "Whatever shall we do? The nightwatch cat is certain to think we're thieves. We shall be taken away, and then he'll look for Jason and Oliver, and they'll get caught, and . . ."

Surprisingly, Topaz, who was often whimpery in a crisis, now rose magnificently to the occasion. "Leave it to me," she mewed softly. "I have a plan."

The nightwatch cat came walking along the alley, swinging a short wooden truncheon. He was a large and solid animal, with glinting eyes and long drooping whiskers which gave him the look of being tigerish and fierce. He stopped and gazed at Calico and Topaz.

"Hello, what's this?" he boomed. "Lurking about, are you?"

Calico could say nothing. Topaz, however, bounced up to him in her dancing way, just as though she hadn't a care in the world. "Oh, *good*," she cried. "Here's a kind gentleman, Auntie. He can direct us, surely."

Auntie indeed, thought Calico sourly. *That was a new one.* But she decided not to interfere.

"Where to, miss?" the nightwatch cat said. "What would you be looking for, now?"

"My aunt and I," Topax said politely, "are up from the country for a few days and we are attempting to find a cat boo-*teek*, sir. You know, where they sell jewelry and suchlike. Not for auntie, of course. She is middle-aged, as you will readily observe. It's for me. I, Topaz. We've come to London especially, well, *nearly* especially, to shop."

"Would you be meaning a place like *The Persian Room,* miss?" the nightwatch cat asked. "Don't know if you'd call it a boutique or not, but it handles a nice line of bells and baubles and bows. All the best lady cats around here go to it."

"The Persian Room!" sighed Topaz dreamily. "It sounds heavenly. Just the sort of place my aunt and I have been trying to find. Could you show us the way, sir?"

"Nothing easier," the nightwatch cat said. "It's about time for my tea break anyway."

He led the way, and Topaz trotted light-pawed behind him, while Calico followed at a slight distance, amazed that Topaz had succeeded in getting him away from the window of Nicolette's.

Had Jason overheard? Would he realize that she and Topaz would return as soon as they safely could?

"Here we are," the nightwatch cat said at last, pointing to a packing case which stood in a deserted corner of the alley. From the outside, it looked only like a large wooden box with a wooden lid. But, as the nightwatch cat led them around to the side of the box, Topaz and Calico noticed a small door, a door which would never be noticed by human eyes. They stepped inside, and there it was: The Persian Room. Topaz and Calico oohed and aahed in admiration and delight.

The floor was carpeted with a piece of Persian rug, softly colored in shades of rose and deep blue and patterned with strange zigzag lines. From the ceiling came a dim pink glow from a dozen little bronze lamps, beautifully decorated with designs of spiderwebs, and suspended from bronze chains. Tastefully displayed were all the things The Persian Room sold: velvet neck-ribbons of every color, peach, scarlet, leafy green; bracelets of silver, finely etched with moons and stars; brass bangles and oriental beads; little turquoise bells that jangled musically. A number of cats, ranging from elderly tabbies to girl cats no older than Topaz, were examining the jewelry and ribbons, trying on neckbands, gazing at bracelets just the right size for a cat's paw. There were three shop assistants, and all were young fluffy white Persian cats.

"Oh, Calico, "Topaz breathed, "how gorgeous! But we'll

never be able to afford anything here. It all looks terrible expensive."

"Well, now that we're here, we may as well look around." Calico replied. "Come along, my dear."

"There's the owner of the shop, over there," the nightwatch cat said, grinning. "Her name's Madame Amina. You go and have a word with her. I'll wait here. I feel a bit out of place among all these fol-di-rols."

Madame Amina was larger and plumper than her shop assistants, but she, too, appeared to be a white Persian. Around her neck she wore a gold necklace with tiny golden coins attached to it. She also wore a pair of pink-framed spectacles which gave her a look of great elegance and charm. Rather timidly, Topaz approached her.

"Excuse me, Madame Amina," she said, "but we were wondering if you might possibly have a neck-ribbon or perhaps a bracelet, for a cat of limited means, such as myself?"

Calico nudged her. "I think we might dip into the Silver Reserve, little T," she whispered. "After all, this is an emergency. We've got to keep the nightwatch cat here long enough for Jason to rescue Oliver."

Madame Amina replied to Topaz haughtily and yet with an air of politeness and courtesy. "Why, of course, Modom," she said in a high tinkling voice. "I'm certain we can find something to please you."

"What did she call me?" Topaz hissed to Calico.

"Modom," Calico hissed back, laughing. "She means madame. Supposed to make her sound ever so posh."

"She scares me a little," Topaz said in a very low voice. "She's so fancy and I'm so ordinary."

"Nonsense, my dear," Calico said. "Appearances count for nothing."

Madame Amina was sorting through a counter full of bells and bangles. She came back with a miniature silver bell on a silver chain and slipped it around Topaz's neck. She then stood back to admire the effect, and held up a large round mirror so Topaz could see herself.

"Ah," Madame Amina cried. "Simply perfect! With your coloring, it blends so beautifully. It's *you*, modom!"

Topaz did not really like the bell all that much, but she felt shy about saying so to the very grand-looking owner of The Persian Room. "Well, . . ." she stammered. "I mean—that is . . ."

At that moment, the nightwatch cat sauntered in. He had been watching the proceedings from the doorway. He put a friendly paw on Madame Amina's shoulder. "Hello, Sal," he said. "How's tricks?"

Madame Amina looked up, startled, and then the haughty expression on her face gave way to a broad smile. She turned aside to speak to him so that the others would not hear. But Calico and Topaz did hear.

"Mikey, as ever was!" she exclaimed in quite a different voice from the one she had used before. "Well, haven't seen you in an age, Mike. Must be months since you last dropped in here. How are you? You're looking well. Hush, though, about the name, luv. Have you forgotten? It doesn't do, not here."

"It's all right," the nightwatch cat said. "These two ladies are friends of mine. I showed 'em the way to your shop, Sal."

"Well, I never," said Madame Amina. "Like to come into the back room for a cuppa tea, all of you?"

Soon they were settled with cups of steaming tea in Madame Amina's private sitting room at the back of the shop.

"Perhaps we better explain," Madame Amina said. "Mike, here, and I grew up together. Knew each other as youngsters, we did."

The nightwatch cat chuckled. "Madame Amina was known as Brixton Sal in those days," he said. "Well, you've worked hard, Sal, and you've got a nice little business here now. Pity about the bleach job, though. I liked you better when you were a plain yellow-furred alley cat."

"What?" said Topaz, astonished. "You mean—you mean you're not a Persian, Madame Amina?"

The older cat smiled. "No, luv, not a trace of the old Persian aristocrat about me. But when I set up the shop and decided to call it The Persian Room and to hire Persian young lady cats for assistants—well, I had to match, didn't I? I've got a wonderful fur-dresser. She didn't have a speck of trouble bleaching me. Of course, I have to go regularly for a touch-up and fluffing, to keep me looking this way!"

Topaz looked rather shocked, but Calico burst out laughing. "It's as I always say," she said. "Appearance is only fur-deep. But I have to admit that I admire you, Madame Amina. You have a lovely shop, and you yourself present a most distinguished appearance."

"How kind of you to say so," Madame Amina purred. "And now, what about something for the young lady, here? Choose whatever you like, luv. It's on the house. I've been a cat of limited means myself, and I know how it feels not to be able to afford even one neck-ribbon."

Topaz began to clap her paws together joyously, but Calico shook her head. "That's very generous, Madame Amina," she said, "but we couldn't possibly. You see, we do have a Silver Reserve."

With that, she produced one of the silver threepennies. Madame Amina and the nightwatch cat looked at it, and the latter whistled. "Whew! That's worth a good deal, I'd say."

"Worth far too much for one of my puny items of jewelry," Madame Amina said firmly. "No, if you insist on paying, it must be much less than that. Here, I tell you what I'll do. That ribbon and bow you're wearing around your neck, little one—I like the design and I'd like to have it copied. I'm sure that sort of bow would sell very well to the younger set. If you'll just allow me to take a sketch of it, you can choose any necklace you want from the shop. You'll be doing me a favor."

Calico had a shrewd suspicion that it was really Madame Amina who was doing Topaz the favor, but she nodded her head in agreement. So Madame Amina sketched the design, and then she and Topaz tripped off and spent quite a few minutes in looking at every necklace in The Persian Room. Finally Topaz chose one with a silver chain and a pendant made of a polished green stone. She spun around, gazing in the mirror, admiring herself.

"Look at me, Calico!" she cried. "Isn't it bee-oo-tiful? Doesn't it suit me? Don't I look too lovely for words? Here, put my old neck-ribbon away, for now, in your bag. Oh, aren't I glamourous?"

"Very pretty," Calico said. "But don't let it go to your head."

"It's not worn on my head, silly," Topaz retorted, although she knew quite well what Calico meant.

Calico's mind was elsewhere. She had been wondering about Jason and Oliver. It seemed now like a betrayal of the nightwatch cat's friendliness, not to tell him of their predicament.

"Mr—er—Mike," she began, somewhat hesitantly. "You've been very kind to us, and so has your friend Madame Amina. We have two small friends here—um—not cats, that is, but a mole and an owl, actually, and they are in serious trouble. Would you mind awfully if we told you about it?"

"Of course I wouldn't mind," the nightwatch cat said heartily. "Carry on. Perhaps I could be of some slight assistance."

Calico, not certain how the story would be received, or whether the nightwatch cat would believe her words, related Oliver's plight and Jason's brave attempt at a rescue.

When she had finished Mike looked worried. "Pity I didn't know all of that before," he said. "Although, to tell you the truth, if you'd rushed up and told me when I was doing my rounds this evening, I don't think I'd have believed you. Too sudden, like. Better this way. But I'm afraid your two friends are going to have to make their escape by themselves—all of us are too large to get in that hole in the window, and there's no other way in. What bothers me is what'll happen if they're seen by a human. Come on. We'd better get back there. At least we can stand guard."

107

Topaz and Calico said good-by to Madame Amina, and thanked her once again. Then they followed Mike out into the alley.

Meantime, while the cats had been visiting The Persian Room, Jason had been working desperately, working against time. He did not know that the nightwatch cat would ultimately prove to be friendly. He believed he had only a few minutes in which to free Oliver and get out again before the cats returned. How was he to do it? He could feel his heart thudding more noisily than usual. The back part of Nicolette's was dark, which was fortunate for him, but Jason knew that soon he would have to face the blinding spotlights in the window where Oliver was held prisoner. He got out his sunglasses and held them in his paws, ready to put on.

Swiftly and silently, Jason raced through the back room where the tea kettle and cups and account books were kept. Swiftly and silently he made his way into the main part of the shop, across the thick soft carpets, past counters containing jewelry and silk scarves and handbags, until he came to the display window. Quickly placing his sunglasses on, Jason sized up the situation. The display window was too high for him to climb up to it.

"Oliver, I'm here," he called.

"Jason!" Oliver said in a relieved voice. "I thought you'd never get here. Hurry, can't you? This cage is driving me crazy. I can't stand being shut up. It goes against my nature. It gives me claustrophobia. That's a word my Gran picked up and gave to me, and I've always been a shade proud of it. It means you can't stand being shut up. Not *shut up* in a talking sense, you understand, although I don't much like that, either. *Shut up* in a cage sense. I get this dizzy hammering inside my head. It's really unbearable. Oh, Jason, I've been so miserable."

Jason tried not to feel annoyed at Oliver for rambling on like this while he, Jason, was trying with all his brain to work out a plan of escape. Oliver had been lonely and frightened, after all, and it was only natural that he should want to talk now. All the same, the chatter bothered Jason and made it difficult for him to concentrate.

"Oliver," he ventured, "would you mind being a little more quiet for a moment, so I can think? The display window is too high; I don't know how to get up."

"Idiotic me!" Oliver cried remorsefully. "Burbling on like a babbling brook. Yakking like a yoke of yokels. Gossiping like a gaggle of geese. How will I ever learn to be wise? How will I ever learn to shut this ever-open beak of mine and seek perfect silence, even sometimes? How . . ."

Jason grinned. Good old Oliver! He really couldn't help it.

He went right on talking, no matter what. Jason's brain began to clear and he discovered he could think after all. Beside the display window stood a white chair with a white and gold striped cushion. Slowly, he climbed onto the rungs and from there he dragged himself up, inching along, until he reached the seat of the chair. Now, with luck, one great leap would do it.

"How do things look outside?" he asked Oliver. "Are there many humans about? Anyone watching?"

"A couple just passing by," Oliver reported. "Now they're gone. Coast clear, Jason!"

Jason summoned all his courage. One-two-three—go! He jumped as forcefully as he could from the chair cushion, away out into the air. To his amazement, he landed successfully on the platform of the display window. Could this really be himself, Jason, attempting a bold rescue? It hardly seemed possible. But surprising things could happen in Thither, even to him.

"Hurrah!" shouted Oliver.

But the end was not yet in sight. Jason still had to climb up the high wicker stand in order to reach the brass cage where Oliver was pacing to and fro.

"I shall have to climb up paw over paw," he said. "I haven't much head for heights, Oliver, I should warn you. Well, here goes."

He repeated to himself his own private motto: *I will try*.

Then he began the long climb, hoping no one would look in the window and notice him. Up, up, up went Jason, up the long slippery pole, quarter inch by quarter inch, as slow as a snail and as nervous as a gnat, but still climbing steadily.

At last he was there. Jason could hardly believe it, but there he was, climbing onto the bars of the cage itself.

"The cage door is around here," Oliver told him. "It's got a latch. If you can manage to lift that, then I'm free."

Slowly and carefully, Jason edged his way around until he came to the cage door. Feeling very unsafe at this height, he

reached up with both his paws and lifted the latch. The cage door swung open, with Jason still clutching onto it.

"Help!" he shrilled. "I'm stuck in mid-air!" He felt small and foolish and terrified. He did not feel like captain, nor at that moment did he believe that it had been such a good idea to come on a quest at all. How could he hope to find a cure for Molanium in this huge city, filled with cages and cars and confusion? Jason quavered inwardly. Maybe all they would find would be trouble and more trouble.

"Don't worry," Oliver said calmly. "I'll fly out and hover close to you, and you can climb on my back. Ready?"

Hoping against hope that no passer-by would see them and raise the alarm, Oliver darted out of the cage and swooped close to Jason, who leaped quickly onto the owl's back. The sudden weight made Oliver veer, and he plunged downward. He managed to right himself, and soon they had landed safely on the carpet of the boutique floor. Then they heard human voices outside the shop.

"That's odd. I thought there was a bird in that cage when we passed by earlier," a woman's voice said.

"I expect they've taken it home for the night," a man's voice replied.

Jason and Oliver looked at one another and began to laugh with relief.

"Quick, now," Jason said. "We must get out before the nightwatch cat returns."

They hurried across the shop and through the back room. The hole in the window, very fortunately, did not need to be enlarged for Oliver, and Jason was reminded of the time when Oliver managed to squeeze through the tunnels of Molanium. By breathing shallowly and flattening his feathers as much as possible, Oliver managed to squirm through. Jason followed, and the two of them hid behind a dust bin just as Calico and Topaz came along the alley, accompanied by the nightwatch cat. Topaz's sharp eyes had caught a glimpse of them.

"It's all right," she called. "Yoo-hoo, Oliver! Jason! Come out, come out, wherever you are. The nightwatch cat is Mr. Mike and he's friendly and so's his friend Madame Amina at The Persian Room and I've got a wonderful necklace and—oh, Oliver, I'm so glad you're out of that cage!"

Jason and Oliver were confused by all this, and refused to come out from behind the dust bin, until Calico explained the whole thing in her sensible way.

"I must say, young fellow," the nightwatch cat said, "you've carried out a heroic rescue. I wouldn't have believed it possible."

Heroic. Jason's heart swelled with pride for a moment. Then he shook his head. "It wasn't heroic," he said. "I was frightened half to death all the time."

"Well, you'd be mighty strange if you hadn't been," Mike said. "But it's how you acted that I'm talking about. Now I must be off and finish my rounds. I'm glad to have met you all, and I wish you luck."

They watched him as he made his way down the alley, singing his nightwatching song and waving his wooden truncheon.

Thieves and robbers had better scat,
Here comes the mighty nightwatch cat!

"I'm glad we told him the whole story," Calico said. "But he was quite right. He'd never have believed us if we'd told him the moment he first came along the alley. He had to get to know us a little, you might say. I think I should tell you, Jason and Oliver, that it was Topaz who had the idea of asking him the way to a cat boutique. Topaz, my dear, you were splendid."

"It was quite easy," Topaz said. "I really did want to do a little shopping, after all."

"I'd like to see that human hag's face when she finds the cage empty tomorrow morning," Oliver said. "Mr. Mike was right, Jason, it was wonderful, the way you rescued me. Really valorous, you were. And Topaz, you were tops."

"You know," Topaz said happily, "I'm rather glad I came

on this expedition after all. And what's more, I've just thought of the words for *Bash On*. Want to hear?"

As they strolled out of the alley and along the narrow twisting streets, Topaz taught the words to them and they all sang:

> *Bash on! Bash on in majesty!*
> *And thwart the fouling churls!*
> *We will not go sedate and slow!*
> *We'll live in swoops and swirls!*

The night was only half over, and they all had the feeling that they would have another adventure before dawn. As it happened, this feeling proved to be quite true.

(5)

BEWARE THE BLADES

"Look," Jason said, pointing to a motorcycle which was parked on the road at the pavement edge.

They all looked, and they saw that there was quite a large basket fastened onto the back. Furthermore, the basket was empty.

"I have the strangest feeling," Jason confessed. "It seems to me that the basket on that motorbike is meant for us to jump into and go for a ride. Perhaps I'm being foolish."

"No, you're not," Topaz said enthusiastically. "Oh, let's go, Jason! I've never had a ride on a motorbike, and I'd love to."

"Take care your new necklace doesn't get blown off," Oliver told her. "It'll be windy, riding in that basket."

Somehow everyone seemed to be taking it for granted that they would go for a ride. Jason hoped his hunch was going to lead them in the right direction. He also hoped that the owner of the motorbike wouldn't look in the basket.

In they hopped, and found that the basket was just big enough to hold them all. A few minutes later, a young man and a girl approached and stopped beside the motorcycle. The four friends held their breaths and tried to scrunch down further into the basket. But the two humans did not even glance at them. The boy climbed onto the motorcycle and the girl got on behind him.

"I thought it was a rotten film, myself," the boy was saying, "but I'm glad you enjoyed it. Come on, let's go and see Angelo."

"Who's he?" the girl asked.

"You know, the chap I told you about," the boy said. "Owns a shop on the Portobello Road."

Portobello Road! The four stowaways in the basket wondered where that was, and what, if anything, would happen to them there.

Voom! Voom! Vrooom! The motorcycle tore along the streets, and in the basket the four friends hung on tightly, so as not to be blown right out of the basket by the force of the wind. What would his mother and sisters think, Jason wondered, if they could see him now? What would the Venerable Mole think? Everything was such a contrast to the slow-moving and indeed, sluggish life of Molanium. For a moment Jason felt a flurry of panic at going so speedily towards he knew not what. Then, as

117

the wind ruffled his smooth black fur, he began to enjoy the sensation. They were traveling towards something exciting. He was sure of it. Maybe this time he would succeed in finding someone who knew about the invisible sickness and how to cure it.

After what seemed like hours of whizzing along roads among honking and hooting cars, they finally stopped. The boy and girl got off the motorcycle and walked away. The four friends, who had found the journey exciting but somewhat bone-rattling, stayed quietly in the basket for a moment or two. When they felt like themselves once more, they crawled out, examined themselves for bruises, decided they were none the worse for their ride, and began to look around them.

On every side they saw shops filled with fascinating objects: old dueling pistols; great curved sabers in finely decorated leather cases; uniforms from regiments who fought in long-ago battles; huge, dark, oil paintings in ornate gilt frames; pictures of spirited horses or portraits of frowning gentlemen; pieces of antique furniture, carved chests and spindly chairs and shining mahogany tables; old jewelry of all sorts and sizes, rings and brooches and necklaces, some set with gleaming amethysts or blue and milky moonstones, some glowing with pale green jade, some bearing mosaics in patterns of roses and forget-me-nots, some heavy and rich with silver or gold.

All the human shops were shut now, as it was well past midnight. The friends walked along the pavement, peering in shop windows. They wondered if there were any shops for their type of creatures in this area, for usually when the human shops shut at night, the shops belonging to what may be termed the Smaller Animals open up and do most of their trade.

They had just begun to give up hope of finding any such shops, when they noticed a young mouse sidling up to them.

"Excuse me," the mouse said timidly, "but I couldn't help noticing you. Would you, by any chance, be looking for the *other* shops?"

"Why, yes," Jason replied. "There are some around here, then?"

"Oh, tons of 'em," the young mouse replied breezily, losing his shyness. "The Portobello Road is famous for its Smaller Animals' shops. Depends on what you're looking for, though, which way you should go. Fish and chips, is it? Antique furniture? Jewelry, new or second hand, real or fake? Opera cloaks? Fancy dress? Theatrical costumes and stage equipment?"

"Jewels!" Topaz burst out. "Let's go and look at jewels! How would I look in a diamond tiara, Calico? Wouldn't I look like the Queen of Everywhere?"

"Sh," Calico said quickly. "It's up to the captain. I think he's got an idea."

"How did you know?" Jason asked.

"Saw it in your face, my dear," Calico said. "A moment ago when this young mouse was telling about the different kinds of shops. Come now, what is it?"

"Well . . ." Jason said hesitantly, not wanting the others to think he was being stupid, "I don't exactly know why, but I think we should go and look at the theatrical costumes. I mean, if that's all right with the rest of you."

"Theatrical costumes!" Oliver snorted. "What for? You're not thinking of going on the stage, are you, Jason?"

"I think Jason's got a reason," Calico said.

"As a matter of fact," Jason admitted, "I did have a sort of idea that we might buy a little something for Mrs. Weepworthy."

"Excellent," Calico said. "I knew you had a reason."

Jason did not mention that he really had another reason as well, because his other reason was too vague to be spoken. He simply felt in some mysterious way that at the theatrical costume shop he would find something he would need, something connected with the quest. But he could not even guess what it might be.

"The place you want to go, then," the young mouse said, "is *The Mole Hole.*"

"The *what?*" they all chorused in amazement.

"The Mole Hole," the mouse repeated. "Owned by an old mole, it is. Don't find many moles these days in the city, but this one's been here for years. C'mon. This way."

They followed the mouse and in a short time they were standing beside a round gatelike hole at the base of an antique furniture shop.

"Right down there," the mouse said. "Follow the tunnel. You can't miss it."

They thanked the mouse and proceeded down the tunnel. Finally they emerged into a small room. Suspended from the ceiling was a hand-painted sign.

THE MOLE HOLE

Theatrical Costumes   *Stage Scenery*

HIRE OR BUY

PRICES ROCK BOTTOM

Digger O'Bucket, Proprietor

All around were costumes: dresses of lace and velvet, old-fashioned breeches and doublets, clown suits, top hats and evening dress, Japanese kimonos of silk and brocades. Among the costumes stood a white-whiskered old mole with spectacles on his nose and a clay tobacco pipe in his mouth.

"Top o' the morning to you," he began cheerfully. Then he noticed Jason. "Sure, if it isn't a mole lad! Don't see many of us around these parts nowadays. Welcome, welcome."

"Thank you," Jason said. "May we look around? We're looking for a present for a friend. A mole lady who used to be on the stage."

"Are you, indeed?" Digger O'Bucket said curiously. "Well, myself having spent near a lifetime on the stage, I wonder if I'd ever have heard of her?"

"Her name is Mrs. Weepworthy," Jason said.

"Weepworthy?" the old mole mused. "No, I don't believe I know it. Of course, she may have been before my time. Or after my time, for that matter, for haven't I been retired these many years? Well, never mind. I just wondered."

Then Jason remembered. He pulled out Mrs. Weepworthy's card and handed it to Digger O'Bucket.

"Of course, Mrs. Weepworthy wasn't her stage name . . ." he began.

He was interrupted by a loud yell from the old mole. "Begorrah, 'tis herself! The loveliest one of them all! Glitter La Fay. By all the stars in the sky and on the stage, 'tis Glitter of the golden voice! Ah, the most beautiful mole lady anyone ever set eyes upon."

"You mean you knew her?" Jason asked, hardly able to believe his ears.

"Knew her?" Digger O'Bucket boomed. "Sure, wasn't she me first love? Did we not sing together with the old M and M— the Mouse and Mole Troupers—in the *Mousedrome,* in the marvelous bygone days when music hall was really music hall? Was not Digger O'Bucket known as The Great Irish Baritone, or as some preferred it, The Shamrock Splendor? Had I not begun by sweeping out the stalls at the Mousedrome, hoping for a chance one day to sing? Was me great talent not recognized one fine day by none other than Glitter La Fay herself, then only a slip of a mole girl? And did we not sing, in unison and in harmony, the most touching version of *When Cathleen Mole Is Smiling* ever to be heard on the stage of the immortal Mousedrome? Ah, I can hear it yet . . ."

With this, Digger O'Bucket burst into song:

(T U N E : *Irish Eyes*)

When Irish moles are digging,
They could dig the world away.
When the Irish moles are dancing,
Even earthworms stop to play.
When Irish moles are singing,
They could charm the birds and trees.
But when Cathleen Mole is smiling,
Sure, the world falls on its knees!

He ended with a magnificent flourish, waving his white clay pipe in one paw. Then, as though demented, he spun around and seized Jason by the shoulder.

"Where is she? Where? Did she not disappear to play the Brighton stage? Was I not unceremoniously shipped off by an ungrateful management to play the provinces? Did I not lose her forever? Don't I still faithfully read the *Smaller Stage and Song,* the magazine of our folk's entertainment world, hoping to see Glitter's name? But all I ever see is names like Perdita and suchlike. Is she in London, boyo? Tell me, quick!"

Jason struggled to get free of Digger O'Bucket's grasp. "It's all there on the card," he said hastily. "Her address. Near Leicester Square. She is a widow, Mr. O'Bucket. Please let go my shoulder."

"Ah, lad, forgive me roughness!" Digger O'Bucket cried. "Sure, 'tis the Irish in me. A passionate people, we Irish, much given to emotional display and suchlike. A widow, you say? Do you think—give me your considered opinion, now—is there a chance she might like to see me? Ah, maybe not, after all these years, me having changed and her also."

Calico, Topaz, and Oliver, not being moles, had remained silent. But now Calico's practical good sense told her to speak.

"Of course she'd like to see you," she said. "She's very lonely, as a matter of fact, and if you asked her to marry you, I believe she'd say *Yes.*"

Digger O'Bucket danced in a sprightly fashion around The Mole Hole, giving a reasonable imitation of an Irish jig.

"I'm off to Leicester Square, this very evening, this very moment!" he cried.

"What a pair they'll make," Topaz whispered to Oliver,

"warbling ancient songs all day. What a din. Never mind; it's quite romantic all the same."

Digger O'Bucket was about to rush out the door when Jason caught his paw and stopped him.

"Wait," Jason begged. "You've forgotten. We came to get a gift for Mrs. Weep—I mean, for Madame La Fay."

"Of course, of course, how stupid of me," Digger O'Bucket said apologetically. "Now let me see . . ."

He began rumaging through shelves and boxes. Finally he came back holding an ivory fan exquisitely enameled with moss roses. It was exactly the right size for a mole lady.

"It's perfect," Topaz pronounced. "She'll love it."

They were all inclined to take Topaz's word on matters of fashion, so they decided to buy the fan. They insisted on giving Digger O'Bucket one of the silver threepennies, although the old stager protested that he didn't want any money from them.

"Very well," he said to Jason, after some argument, "you shall pay me for the fan, and I'll deliver it to Glitter with your compliments. But now, boyo, you must accept something from me."

Jason was about to protest politely, when he felt a tingling around the rim of the Cap Of Deeper Thinking, which he had pulled down around his ears earlier on, so it would not get blown off on the motorcycle ride. He began thinking very quickly and seriously. It seemed to him that this was the other reason he had wanted to come to The Mole Hole, and that whatever Digger O'Bucket's gift might be, it was important for all of them that he, Jason, should accept it. Before he could say a word, however, Digger O'Bucket said something that mirrored Jason's own thoughts.

"Sure, something *told* me I shouldn't sell this particular article. Had a fine offer for it day before yesterday, but I turned it down. The Irish, you know, have the talent of second sight, sometimes. It's as though I knew you'd be along, boyo. I have a notion this'll be of some use to you in your travels."

With that, he went to a dresser, opened the bottom drawer, and drew something out, a sticklike something. Jason was convinced that it was a sword, and for an instant he felt a terrible uncertainty. He was not, he knew in his heart of hearts, much of a creature for swords.

"There you are," Digger O'Bucket said. "Have you ever, in your born days, seen a more handsome umbrella?"

Umbrella! Jason felt himself blushing with embarrassment. It was extremely kind of Digger O'Bucket, but what possible use was an umbrella? Of course, one could put it up in case of rain, but Jason's habit, when it rained really hard, was simply to seek shelter and wait. Showers didn't bother him. In fact, he rather liked them.

"Thanks very much indeed," he murmured.

Digger O'Bucket was chortling. "Oho," he said, "you're thinking what a daft thing the old codger's giving you, aren't you, now? Wait, now, me lad. Take a good look at it."

They all looked closely at the umbrella. It was pale, leaf-green silk, and it had a handle of bronze, embossed with strange signs and symbols which none of the four friends could read, for it seemed to be another language. It was certainly an exceptional-looking umbrella, but it was still only an umbrella.

Then Digger O'Bucket opened it up. Instantly, a small propeller sprang out from the topmost tip, above the green silk. Inside, attached to the upper part of the handle, Jason could see a square black box, tiny and compact, with several neat round knobs on it.

"What is it?" he cried, overwhelmed with curiosity.

Digger O'Bucket smiled triumphantly. "This is the world's one and only Flying Umbrella," he explained. "An eccentric mole inventor made it some years back, and it came into my hands through a series of events too complicated to relate here and now. Sure, and doesn't it work like a helicopter, now? When you turn this little bit of a knob here, the propeller starts whirling at colossal speed, and the umbrella takes off, and you with it, boyo. Take the word of Digger O'Bucket. Indeed, and to be sure, and the saints be praised, it takes off and flies like a pretty green bird."

They all crowded around to get a better look.

"What a useful object, my dears," Calico said. "Although I can't imagine myself ever wanting to fly, mind you."

"Oo! Can I try it, Jason?" Topaz purred. "Please let me. I'll be ever so careful."

"No," Jason decided. "I think it must be saved for a real emergency. I think that's what we're meant to do with it."

"I always maintained that air travel was superior to any other kind," Oliver said with satisfaction. "Just wait, Jason, until you're zooming along in the sky—you'll see what a pleasure it is."

Jason shut the Flying Umbrella, rolled it up carefully, and held it tightly in one paw. "I can never thank you enough," he said to the old mole.

"T'was nothing," Digger O'Bucket said. "Sure, wasn't it merely waiting here for you to claim it? And now, if you'll excuse me, I think I'll shut the shop, for I'm off to Leicester Square to seek me darlin' Glitter La Fay."

They said a warm farewell to the Great Irish Baritone. Then they went through the tunnel and emerged onto the Portobello Road once more. They walked along slowly, looking for a place to spend the day.

All at once, Calico gave a startled gasp. "Look, my dears, just across the street there. Are my eyes deceiving me, or is it *those two?*"

They looked and, sure enough, there were the two ominous mice they had encountered in Covent Garden when they first arrived in London. Jacko and Charlie were slinking quietly along, still wearing their wide black leather belts with buckles shaped

like B's. Attached to each belt was a wicked-looking knife. The mice were staring directly at the four friends.

Jason felt a peculiar sinking sensation in the pit of his stomach. The mouse, Jacko, put one paw to his teeth and gave a piercing whistle. Then, before the four friends had time to realize what was happening, the street was suddenly filled with large lean mice and rats, each smirking evilly and each wearing a black belt and knife.

"Run!" shouted Jason. "Quick! They're after us!"

Too late. The four were surrounded. Instinctively, they drew close together, and this was the worst thing they could have done, for within seconds a tall yellow-fanged rat had flung a rope lariat around them and had drawn the noose. There they were, held around their middles, all in a heap. A dozen rats and mice scurried

up with a large canvas bag, and the four friends were shoved inside. The drawstring on the bag was tightened, and they could feel rat and mouse claws grabbing at the canvas and beginning to drag it along the pavement.

"Murder! Help! Police!" screeched Topaz, who was frightened nearly out of her wits.

"Hush, my dear," soothed Calico. "We're in a sticky situation, and no mistake, but let's not get hysterical."

Oliver tried to flap his wings and found he could not even do that, as they were tightly held by the rope.

"Can't stand this, I can't," he gulped. "First a cage and now a canvas bag. I want out! Villains! Highwaymen!"

Jason was silent, for one good reason. He was shaking so much that he was afraid he would only stutter if he spoke. He did everything he could think of to calm himself. He touched the golden pompom of the Cap Of Deeper Thinking, and reminded himself that the Venerable Mole had trusted him enough to give him the cap to wear. He felt for the Flying Umbrella, and it was still there under his arm. By this time, his teeth had almost stopped chattering with fear. All the same, he wished someone else were captain.

"L-let's try to c-consider," he began, stammering only a trifle. "First, where are we being taken, and why? Second, who is taking us there?"

"How do we know where we're being taken?" Topaz asked sobbing. "To a dark dungeon, if you ask me. No one will ever see me in my lovely necklace again. Oh, the waste! And me so young!"

"Do at least *try*, little T," Calico said sternly.

"I'm sorry," Topaz sniffed. "I will try, then. For one thing, Jason, it's perfectly obvious that we're in the hands of some widespread criminal organization."

Jason looked at her in wonder. How was it that she could be

so frivolous or weepy one minute, and the next minute come out with the words to a new song or some quite shrewd observation such as the one she had just made? In a way, it was like Oliver, whose constant talk and tactlessness could be annoying, but who was always there when you needed him and whose generosity was unfailing. Or Calico, who could seem so strict and dignified and disapproving, and yet could comfort and help all of them in moments of crisis. Or me, for that matter, Jason thought. Always a bit afraid (not to say petrified) in time of danger, yet managing to go on somehow. All of them were mixtures.

"You're right, Topaz," he said. "That's it. Why didn't we see it before? It's some kind of gang. But why are they out to get *us?*"

At that moment, the canvas sack stopped moving. There was a high angry squeaking of mice and rats, and then Jacko's voice: "C'mon, you Blades. Onto the truck with this lot, before the driver gets back, or else we've had it."

Scrunch—scrunch—scrunch! The sack was being dragged up a wooden platform of some kind. Silence for a few minutes. Then a human voice: "Okay, mate. That's the last of the coal sacks. I'm off now. See you later."

The platform, clearly, was the back of a truck, now being lifted and slammed by the driver. The mice and rats must have loaded them onto a vehicle going in some known direction, Jason realized. He thought hard. Dawn had not yet come. The truck driver must be on night duty, just like the truck that first carried them into London. Jason had begun to understand that some of the big trucks moved mainly at night to avoid blocking the daytime traffic. But where could they be going now?

With a deep roar of its motor, the truck started up, and soon they were jolting along the road, uncomfortably held by the rope within the canvas bag, bumped and bruised at every turn. All around them, on the outside of the sack, they could hear the squealing and bickering of rat and mouse voices.

The truck groaned to a stop, and at first Jason thought it was just another traffic light. But no.

Jacko's voice rose in command: "Hop to it, Blades! Get 'em off smartly now, before the driver gets back. He takes ten minutes here, on this run, for his tea break, so you better look sharp, or the G.R. will want to know why."

Scrape—scrape—scrape—THUD! The bag with the four friends in it was off the truck and had landed on the pavement of the road. They were all shaken, but no one was seriously hurt.

"All right, get going." It was Jacko speaking once more. "You know what to do with 'em."

134

For an awful moment Jason thought that the rats and mice were going to pull the sack to a deep well or a sewer, and drop them in to drown. Then he felt the sack being taken along another pavement, over rough cobblestones or bricks, and finally, to his intense surprise, the rope around the mouth of the bag was loosened, and the four tumbled out.

Jason blinked and looked around. He saw a large signboard which said TIMES OF DEPARTURE. He saw a sign which said WAITING ROOM, and another which said SNACK BAR. He saw, in the darkness, big white numerals: 1,2,3, and 4, each above a wooden gate. He looked up and saw, high above, steel beams and rafters, and a sloping roof, part of which was strangely paneled in glass. Through the glass panes the starlight was feebly streaking in, shafts of pearl-gray half-light.

"We're in a railway station, I think," Calico said. "Now, keep calm, everyone."

"I'm scared," Topaz whimpered. Then, in quite a brisk voice, she added, "Wait till I get out of this rope; I'll scratch every mouse in sight."

"I think," Oliver whispered very very softly, "that if I wriggle my wings a bit, I can get them free. Then, once I'm out, the rope will be loose enough and you can all get away, too."

"Wait," Jason cautioned. "Loosen your wings now, Oliver, but don't fly yet. Don't let them see we might be able to escape.

135

Not until we've learned who they are, and what they want with us."

The lieutenant mouse, Jacko, and his henchman, Charlie, loomed up near the four, and then they noticed that all the rats and mice had gathered in a circle around them. Jason felt as though he were totally surrounded by evil presences.

"What've you got to say now, eh, brain-boy?"

Jason realized it was Jacko's snarling voice, addressing him. He summoned his strength. He must not stammer. Not here, not now. "We'd like to know," he said distinctly, "just who you are, and why you've captured us, and where we are."

The rows of rats and mice began to laugh, a cruel snickering that rose shrilly in the vast emptiness of the deserted station, which had closed for the night. No humans would be around here for hours, not until early morning. Jason would have welcomed a few humans right now.

"Oh, you would, eh?" Jacko said. "Hear that, Charlie? They'd like to know all about everything. Shall we tell 'em?"

"May as well," Charlie replied. "Best for them to know what they're up against, and that they don't stand a chance."

"Right you are," Jacko agreed. He turned again to the four. "Where you are this minute is Marylebone Station. Nice little old station. Dignified, like. Proper respectable. In daytime, that is. We sometimes borrow it, see, as one of our gathering places, on nights like this, when we've got types like you to deal with. **Right, boys?"**

Shouts of *Right! Jacko's always right!*

"Now, then," Jacko continued, "as to who we are. For your information, we're the Blades. Blades by name, blades by nature, blades by, you might say, profession. Our leader is the Great Rat."

Cries of *Hail, the Blades! Hail, the Great Rat!*

"He's the top brass in this outfit," Jacko went on. "You won't likely ever see him. He's too important to bother with little shrimps like you lot."

"But what have you got against us?" Jason cried. "What have we ever done to you?"

Jacko grinned, showing his pointed teeth. "We've received information," he said. "Information from one of our agents. A cat friend, you might say."

"Winstanley, I'll be bound," Calico spat out.

"That's right, Ma," Jacko said unpleasantly. "Stan's been caught, thanks to you, but he managed to smuggle out a message telling us about your so-called Silver Reserve. That's our first little request. Hand over the lolly. The loot. The silver, to you."

Calico's fur began to spark electrically, and her spine curved in fury.

"Why, you—you . . ."

"Hold it," Jacko said, with a flippant wave of one paw.

"That's not all. You ever heard that jolly old song: *The more we are together, the happier we'll be?* Well, we Blades have a slightly different version: *The more they are apart, the happier we'll be.* The Blades don't like to see cats associating with moles, and moles getting all palsy-walsy with owls. It makes us nervous, see? And when the Blades get nervous, their fingers start getting itchy on their knives, see?"

From the Blades came thunderous yells of *Let's cut 'em up, Jacko!*

"And the reason it makes us nervous," Jacko said, ignoring the clamor, "is that we've got a profitable business going for us, see? We've got clients, as you might say. Protection is our business. Some call it the protection racket, but we prefer the word *business.* Mice pay us to protect 'em from cats, and cats pay us to protect 'em from dogs, and we even have a few cowardly dog clients who pay us to protect 'em from long-clawed cats and from the more ferocious rats (who are mostly Blades, I may say). And so it goes. Therefore, all this chumminess with you lot isn't good for our business, see? Might give all sorts of Smaller Animals the idea that they could get along together, without being scared of each other. That would never do, not for us. So, to cut a long story short, our instructions from the Great Rat are very simple. *Get their silver, Jacko,* he tells me, *and then run 'em out of town. Tell 'em to go home and never come back.* Now, are you going to agree nice and quiet, or do I have to get my Blades to—ah—persuade you?"

"Certainly, we'll agree quietly to anything you say," Jason answered meekly.

Topaz, Oliver, and Calico stared at him in disbelief. Could this be Jason talking?

"Jason, what are you saying?" Calico whispered, "You can't mean it!"

"Of course not," Jason whispered back. "Be ready to act quickly. When I say *Silver Reserve,* that's the signal. Got it?"

They all nodded.

Jason turned to Jacko. "Since we can't possibly win against all of you," he said, "let's begin with the money. Do you want it now?"

"You catch on quick," Jacko said sarcastically, stepping close to Jason.

"Right," Jason said. "Here it is, then. Here's our Silver Reserve."

At those words, Oliver flew, like a flash of storm lightning, directly in Jacko's face, completely knocking the lieutenant mouse over backwards. Topaz took a light-footed leap over the heads of the brigade of Blades. Calico, her fur bristling with battle, bared her claws and raked them across the ranks of rats and mice, who by this time were milling around in confusion.

As for Jason, he did the most remarkable thing of all. Quickly

139

putting up the Flying Umbrella, Jason turned the knob marked *Onward*. Immediately, the propeller at the tip of the umbrella began to turn with a rapid zinging noise. With Jason clinging to the bronze handle, the contraption buzzed and whirled a short distance above the station floor.

Wham! Boing! Kerplunk! Down went the Blades like a row of wooden soldiers, as Jason and the Flying Umbrella careened into them. They soon recovered, however. Jacko was on his feet, shouting at the others, trying to restore order. Soon a dozen of the Blades were up again, wielding their dreadful knives.

Swift as the flick of a fly's wings, Jason turned the knob marked *Upward,* and the umbrella began to rise up, higher and higher. Jason had a brief second of wondering fearfully if he would be able to make the umbrella stop before it crashed into the glass and metal roof of Marylebone Station. Almost at once, however, he noticed the *Off* knob, and knew he would be all right. Then another panic—how to steer?

"Must be this lever here," Jason muttered to himself, concentrating so much that he was hardly aware of the scene below. Sure enough, the lever controlled the steering. Jason soon found that he was able to operate the Flying Umbrella with no trouble at all, and he began to enjoy the floating sensation.

"I'm flying!" he thought, marveling at it. "I, Jason, am really and truly flying."

How incredible it all seemed, and what a long distance he had come from Molanium, where even a short trip to Thither seemed hazardous, much less a journey into the air. Suddenly Jason heard a voice.

"Over here!" It was Oliver. Jason guided the umbrella to the rafter where Oliver was perched, glided down beside the owl, and turned the *Off* knob.

"Oh Oliver," he exclaimed, "it's exactly as you said. There's nothing like flying. What's happened to the cats, though?"

"That's just it," Oliver said in a worried tone. "I can't see them. I don't want to be gloomy, Jason, but I fear the worst."

Together they gazed downward, but not a sign of the cats could they see. They looked and looked, until their eyes felt strained, but Calico and Topaz were nowhere in sight. All they could see was a mass of Blades, now reformed into a small but deadly army, marching grimly around the station as though searching.

"Calico and Topaz haven't been caught yet," Jason said. "Thank goodness for that, anyway. They must be hiding. But where? And how are any of us going to get out of here?"

Just then there was a terrific commotion. At one side of the station, near Platform One, stood a booth with a sign which said: *Photos Completed In 3 Minutes. 4 Poses 2/6. Passport Approved.* In front of this booth was a green curtain, so that human customers could enter and take their own pictures with the camera concealed inside, which would then develop and print the photographs in practically no time at all. No human was inside the booth at this moment, getting his picture taken, but something or someone was certainly there for, as the Blades marched past, the green curtains were abruptly yanked down and flung on top of the rats and mice.

The Blades struggled and squealed, enveloped as they were in the dark folds of the curtains. There were cries of fright from rat and mouse voices. *Must be ghosts! Help, spooks!* Then, one by one, the bedraggled Blades emerged, not slowly, but running on the double, fleeing as fast as their feet would take them, off and away.

The last Blade to appear was Jacko. He did not run. He looked furiously at his gang and shook one paw towards the roof where Jason and Oliver were sitting.

"Ghosts, my eye!" he shouted. "I know who to blame for this."

But there was nothing he could do to persuade his scattered followers to return. With a final snarl, he stamped out of Marylebone Station.

Topaz and Calico, both stepping rather proudly, tails up, came out of the booth and sauntered across the station floor.

"Yoo-hoo!" Topaz called. "You can come down now. The Blades have gone."

"I really can't remember a more satisfactory campaign," Calico remarked in an unruffled voice.

Oliver flew down on his wings while Jason drifted down on the Flying Umbrella. They both congratulated the cats on having dispersed the Blades. For a while, none of the four could do anything except discuss the exciting events which had just happened. Topaz, in a gust of enthusiasm, even discovered a verse to commemorate the occasion:

On Marylebone the moonlight fades;
The night is gone, and so are the Blades.

Unfortunately, something began to nag at the back of Jason's mind. "I don't believe that we've seen the last of the Blades," he said. "And now we have a new problem as well."

"What's that?" the others demanded.

"The Blades know about the Flying Umbrella," Jason said slowly.

"We shall have to guard it," Calico said determinedly, "with our lives."

The others agreed, and began to sing:

Four for One, and One for Four,
Together till the journey's o'er.

Jason felt grateful to have such loyal friends. All of them, after all, had better defenses than he did, in moments of danger. Oliver had wings. The cats had their claws and could also leap wide distances, if need be, to escape. He, Jason, did not have these natural advantages. Yet the others, he knew, would never desert him.

The fact remained that the Flying Umbrella, useful as it might still be, had now lost its surprise value. No longer could a

Blade be caught off guard by it. Then, too, there was the ever-present danger of having it stolen. The dawn was creeping into the sky, and Jason felt too tired to think any more.

"I don't imagine the Blades will return now," he said wearily. "Let's try to find a safe corner here, and get some rest."

"Look," Calico said, pointing. "There's an *Underground* sign. This station leads to an underground train, to take people around London. Why not go down and find a nook to sleep in? Even if the Blades do come back, they'll never think of looking down there."

So, with Oliver bravely overcoming his feeling against deep places, they went down to the platform where the underground trains ran and, despite the rumble of engines both above and below, they all slept soundly throughout the day.

(6)

STRINE, SPICE,

THE PETUNIAS, AND

MOST OF ALL, PERDITA

Jason rubbed his eyes and yawned. The evening was well advanced. He had overslept. The cats and Oliver were already awake. Jason looked out from his hiding place under a bench and saw a great many human feet encased in a great many different kinds of shoes: heavy work boots, slim suede shoes, stout oxfords, ladies' high-heeled shoes, flimsy as flowers. All the feet were hurrying as the people made their way into the underground train that had just come to a stop at this platform.

Jason had an idea. "Listen," he said excitedly to the others, "why don't we try to get on a train? I don't know where it would take us, but at least it would take us somewhere."

"Yes, let's," said Topaz. "I'm longing to have a ride on one of these underground trains."

But Oliver was inclined to disagree. "That's all very well," he said, "but how can two cats, an owl, and a mole get on a train without being noticed by humans? I don't want to end up in another cage, I can tell you."

"I think we'll be safe," Calico said. "I was doing a little exploring, in a quiet way, before the rest of you woke up, and I noticed that the carriages at the very end of the train are often empty. The humans tend to bunch all together in the middle of the platform. So if we creep along to the end of the platform, all we need to do is wait until we see an empty coach. The doors open and close by themselves, so we'll just have to nip in at the right moment."

Oliver still had doubts, but they decided to follow Calico's suggestion. Carefully they made their way to the end of the platform, and when a train came along with an empty coach, they quickly slipped aboard.

Clank! The doors closed, and the train was on its way, through tunnels and into the next station.

"How will we know when to get off?" Oliver inquired, when they had passed several stations.

"Someone must look out at the next stop," Jason said, "and try to see the station sign."

Secretly he hoped one of the others would volunteer. The train doors frightened him. What if he got caught when they were slamming shut? A creature as small as a mole would be crushed completely.

"I'll look," Calico offered. "My eyes are excellent."

At the next stop, therefore, she stood in the open doorway of the train. "Trafalgar Square," she announced.

"That has a splendid sound," said Oliver, who was still very nervous about trains and was anxious to get out. "Let's go and see."

Out they all jumped and at last found their way up to the street. What they saw then was positively dazzling. Great fountains were blossoming in huge white sprays and cascades of water, and around these fountains thronged not only people but hundreds and hundreds of pigeons with feathers of white and gray and soft blue and greenish-purple. On one side of the square was a high column and, by craning their necks and straining their eyes, the four friends could just make out the statue of a man in a military uniform at the very top. At the four corners of the column's broad base were gigantic bronze lions. Oliver flew over to have a better look.

"Lord Nelson," he reported back. "That's who the statue is. Horatio, Lord Nelson, hero of the Battle of Trafalgar. Come on, let's go and park ourselves between a lion's paws. We'll be quite safe there, and we can watch everything going on. The true London at last! Trafalgar Square in the evening! Isn't it tremendously exciting? Can't you feel your blood racing and your pulse pulsing? Wait till my Gran hears about this. I'm beginning to feel like an owl of the world. Look at those millions of pigeons! Fancy spending your life like that, living in the throbbing heart of this mighty city . . ."

"Oliver," Jason interrupted, "I'm sorry to sound discouraging, but how are we going to climb up as far as the bronze lions? They're mounted on the column's base, and they're higher than a human's head."

"That's easy," Oliver replied. "You can zing up on your Flying Umbrella and the cats can take a flying leap when no one's looking. I'll give the signal. After all, I'm meant to be chief of signals, aren't I?"

Jason thought about this plan. It seemed to him that if a human were to observe a mole rocketing upwards on a helicopter-type umbrella, the result might be an unpleasant outcry.

"I don't think it's a good idea for me to use the umbrella," he said. "Only emergencies, remember? I'll hang onto Calico's fur."

So this was what they did. Oliver shouted, "Now!" at a moment when no human eyes were turned in the direction of the bronze lion, and the two cats sprang up onto the dark metal paws. Jason, holding tightly to Calico's neck fur with one paw, and to his umbrella with the other, felt decidedly shaken, but after a second or two he regained his composure and began to enjoy looking around. From this vantage point, he could see the whole square: the strolling humans, the strutting pigeons, the white-foaming fountains. Then Oliver was poking him in the ribs with a wingtip.

"Look, Jason! Right over there, on another bronze lion. Do you see them? Three owls! My own folk. Oh, Jason, what a wonderful moment this is. I can hardly wait to talk with them. London owls *must* be wise, wouldn't you say? At last I've found someone who can tell me how to be a proper owl. I shall go home positively stuffed with wisdom. I just know it!"

With that, Oliver began flapping his wings to attract the attention of the three owls. "Yoo hoo, you over there!" he called. "Come and talk to us!"

The three owls looked up, and when they saw the cats and

Jason, they began to nudge each other and point their wings suspiciously.

"Ugh!" cried the first owl.

"Brr!" cried the second owl.

"Phew!" cried the third owl.

Oliver thought he knew what was bothering them. "It's all right," he explained. "These cats and this mole are friends of mine. Nobody will hurt you. I can guarantee it. We're from the country and we've come to London on a quest, and I can't tell you how glad I am to see some fellow owls. There are all kinds of things I want to ask you."

The three owls gaped, open-mouthed. Then they shook their heads and began to giggle. Not very pleasant laughter, Jason thought. It reminded him of the Blades' mocking laughter, except that these owls did not seem as sharp and sly as the Blades. They seemed—how terrible for Oliver—merely stupid.

"We're not coming over there," the first owl said.

"Fancy traveling about with cats and moles," the second owl said.

"We got nothing to say to you lot," the third owl said.

"Wait a minute," Oliver said desperately. "I'm trying to explain to you. These are my *friends,* and . . ."

"Ugh—ugly," said the first owl.

"Brr—horrible," said the second owl.

"Phew—nasty," said the third owl.

Oliver was deeply embarrassed by this rudeness towards his friends. For once, he could not think of anything to say.

Jason tried to smooth things over. "Well, never mind all that just now," he said. "Perhaps these owls would be kind enough to tell us some of the things we should see in London—the sights, you know. Famous places. Maybe they could point them out on our street maps in the London A to Z book . . ."

The three owls began to hoot.

"Books—ugh!" screeched the first owl.

"Some old geezer tried to teach us to read—Brr!" screeched the second owl.

"But we wouldn't, not us—Phew!" screeched the third owl.

Oliver was sunk in gloom. He could hardly bear to face his friends, so mortified did he feel at the dim-wittedness of these owls. He could say nothing, and the others could not think of any words which would comfort him. Then the three strange owls decided they had had enough of conversation.

"Come on! Let's go and pull that old pigeon's tailfeathers!" the first yelled.

"Whee! That'll annoy him, silly old pigeon!" the second yelled.

"We hate pigeons!" the third yelled.

Oliver regarded them bleakly. "And just why do you hate pigeons," he said. "If I may be so bold as to inquire?"

"We hate pigeons 'cause they're pigeons," the first owl said.

"We hate pigeons 'cause their feathers are gray and blue, not brown like ours," the second owl said.

"We hate pigeons 'cause they ain't owls," the third maintained.

The three owls fluttered down and began tweaking the tailfeathers of a sleeping pigeon. The pigeon's head was tucked under one wing, so they could not see his face, and his feathers were fluffed out, so that he appeared to be a fattish elderly bird. He awoke with a start, held up his head, sleeked down his feathers, and then it became clear that he was not a fattish elderly pigeon but a large and powerful youngish pigeon, now considerably annoyed. With a sweep of his great wings, he rose into the air, his eyes flashing beadily. The three owls realized their mistake. Squawking in terror, they flew away as fast as their smaller wings would carry them.

The large pigeon landed on the bronze lion, just beside the four friends, and began chuckling.

"They'll fly all the way to Regents Park before they realize I'm not still chasing them," he said. "Well, allow me to introduce myself. I'm known as Joey Blue. I wasn't actually sleeping when you were talking with those rascals—only resting, you might say. I'm sorry your introduction to the London owls had to be with Ugh, Brr, and Phew."

"With *what?*" Oliver asked.

"Ugh, Brr, and Phew," the pigeon repeated. "That's what we call 'em, because that's what they're always saying. Empty-headed bunch, they are. Pay no attention to them. Take no notice."

"How can I help taking notice?" Oliver said sadly. "I'd been counting on finding at least a few owls who could tell me how to be wise, but those three couldn't tell anyone the time of day. Why, they said they didn't even want to learn to read!"

"Professor Kingsberry tried," Joey Blue said, "but they couldn't be bothered. Well, lad, don't be upset. If you believed that all owls were wise except yourself, then you're a little wiser already."

"That's true," Oliver admitted. "I guess some are and some aren't. Who is Professor Kingsberry?"

"Who, who, who-oo-oo is Professor Kingsberry?" came an owl voice nearby. "Who, who, who-oo-oo is he? Why, none other than myself! That's who-oo!"

A rather scrawny tawny owl landed beside them. He was neither young nor old, and behind his spectacles they could see his eyes glimmering with humor.

"Good evening, Joey," he said.

"Evening, Prof," Joey Blue replied. "This young owl here, Oliver by name, has a problem, like. Looking for wisdom, it seems, and got quite a shock when he met Ugh, Brr, and Phew."

"Please, sir," Oliver said pleadingly, "are you a genuinely wise owl, at last? My name's Oliver, and I am questing for only one simple thing: someone who can tell me how to be wise."

Professor Kingsberry laughed gently. "I come from a long line of British Museum owls," he said, "and I've been studying there, off and on, for many years now, finding my way in at night, you know, and making use of the Reading Room when the humans aren't there. I've read history and philosophy, science and psychology, music and biology, art and anthropology. But I'm afraid I can't tell you how to be wise, Oliver. That you must learn for yourself. I don't consider myself all that wise, to tell you the truth. Knowledge can be learned from books. But wisdom, now— wisdom must be learned from life itself. I've picked up a little, along the way, perhaps, and I fancy that you have too, young as you are. You must just go on by yourself, and if you have an opinion which turns out to be mistaken, Oliver, don't be afraid to change your mind, will you? Be patient. When you get home, you may be surprised at what you've learned. Now, I must be off for my evening classes—good luck, all!" Professor Kingsberry tipped his wings in courteous farewell and flew away.

"Nice fellow," Joey Blue mused. "Comes to eat his lunch

here quite often, and we get talking. He was an explorer owl, once, in the Amazon jungles. Never think it to look at him, would you?"

"What did he mean: I must go on by myself?" Oliver said hopelessly. "I guess the quest is useless for me. So far the only owls I've met have been those three idiotic ones, and now Professor Kingsberry who may be wise but who says he can't teach me wisdom. I may as well pack up and go home."

"Wait, my dear," Calico put in. "Remember what he said: be patient, and you may be surprised at what you've learned. Anyway, you can't leave us now, Oliver, we need you."

"Oh, well, in that case . . ." Oliver said, looking pleased. "Of course I'll stay. Do *you* think I'm needed, too, Jason?"

"We couldn't get along without a chief of signals, Oliver." Jason said decidedly. "And besides, you're such good company."

"Well, I don't feel any wiser than I ever did," Oliver sighed, "but I guess I'll just keep traipsing along and see what happens."

Jason felt this was a good time to bring up the question of his own part of the quest. He explained everything to Joey Blue, and asked his advice.

"Do you happen to know anything about invisible sicknesses," he inquired, "or could you suggest anyone who might be able to help me find a cure for Molanium?"

Regretfully, Joey Blue shook his head. "I'm sorry," he said, "but I've never in my life heard of the invisible sickness, and I don't think I know anyone who might . . ." He stopped suddenly and rapped one wing against his forehead as though he had just remembered something of importance. "Of course!" Joey cried. "I was forgetting Perdita! That's who you want to look for, Jason!"

"Who under earth is Perdita?" Jason asked, puzzled. The name had a familiar sound, somehow, but he couldn't remember where he had heard it before.

Joey Blue laughed cheerily. "You'll know her when you see her. There's only one Perdita. I can't promise that she'll be able to help, but it's worth a try. You may find her at *The Petunia Patch*."

"The *petunia* patch?" Jason repeated, totally mystified.

"No, no, not a flower garden," the big pigeon said. "It's a club for Smaller Animals and suchlike. On Earls' Court Road. Go by underground. Change at Piccadilly Circus and take the Piccadilly Line to Earls' Court. 'Bye for now, and the best of luck to you. I must stretch my wings a bit. I usually fly up and say hello to Lord Nelson about this time of night."

As the four friends climbed down from the bronze lion and

made their way across Trafalgar Square, they heard the voice of Joey Blue floating down from high in the air, near the top of the Nelson Column.

"Remember the name: Per-deet-ahh!"

The underground journey was perilous, but finally they achieved their destination and found themselves walking along Earls' Court Road. The evening was fine and their spirits were high. They had no idea how they would find The Petunia Patch, or Perdita, whoever she was, but they felt confident it would all work out somehow.

Just as they were beginning to wonder when they would ever encounter someone who could tell them the way, they saw two handsome cats ambling down the street towards them. One cat was ginger and the other was black. The two of them were joking as they walked along, but when they met the four friends, they stopped and gazed curiously.

"Hey, cobber, who's this?" the ginger cat asked the black cat.

"Man, my eyes have not lighted on these folk before this moment." the black cat replied. "They do not live here on the Road, that's certain."

Calico approached politely. "Excuse me, gentlemen," she

158

began. "I wonder if you would be so kind as to tell us how to find a Smaller Animals' club called The Petunia Patch?"

"Nothing easier," the ginger cat answered companionably. "We're going there ourselves."

As they all proceeded along Earls' Court Road, they introduced themselves.

"I'm Calico," said Calico, "and this is Topaz. The young mole with cap and umbrella is Jason, the captain of our group, and the owl is Oliver, our chief of signals."

"Pleased to make your acquaintance," the ginger cat said. "I'm Strine and this is Spice."

"Why do you talk with that peculiar accent?" Topaz wanted to know. "I've never heard anything like it."

"Sh, little T," Calico said. "No rudeness, *if* you please."

"Don't worry, I don't mind what the little cat says," Strine said. "I talk this way because I'm Strine."

"What his meaning is, man," Spice put in, "is that he is Australian."

"I see," Calico said, although, in fact, it wasn't all that clear to her. "But why do you call me *man?* I, sir, am a lady."

Spice roared with deep-throated laughter. "Lord, man, I know that, gal. It just the way the words is coming into my mouth, that's all. It is the way we folk talk back home. That heaven's own truth."

"Where do you come from, then?" Calico asked.

"West Indies," Spice said. "Jamaica is where this cat hail from."

While Spice and Calico were exchanging interesting information about their respective backgrounds, Topaz was talking to Strine.

"I like the way you talk," she said in her open-hearted although perhaps slightly extravagant manner. "I think it is just perfectly marvelous. How do you like my necklace? I got it at a boo-*teek* called The Persian Room. Isn't it elegant?"

"You're a nice looking kitten all right," Strine agreed with a smile.

Then they were there. The Petunia Patch was in the basement underneath an Italian restaurant. Spice tapped three times on a grating in the wall, and a mouse voice answered somewhat timidly: "Who's there?"

"Me, Spice," the black cat replied. "With Strine and some friends."

The grating swung open, revealing narrow steps leading downward.

"Sorry to be fussy," the attendant mouse said, "but we've had a certain amount of bother from you-know-who recently."

"Think nothing of it, man," Spice said, as they began descending the stairs.

"You may know who, but I don't," Calico remarked. "What was he talking about, Spice?"

"Some no-good-niks who are calling themselves The Blades," Spice said, shrugging. "Don't you go bothering your head about it."

"The Blades!" Calico, Topaz, Oliver, and Jason all cried in unison.

"Hey, cobber," Strine said to Spice, "hear that? They know 'em."

"Indeed we do, alas," Calico said. "You tell them, Jason."

So Jason recounted their capture by the Blades, and how they finally overcame the evil force in Marylebone Station. Strine and Spice whistled low.

"My word," Strine said, scratching one ear. "This may be a dicey situation, mates. Didn't know they had their claws into you lot. We're going to have to watch out."

"You don't think they'd come here?" Jason asked anxiously.

"That keen-eyed mouse at the door," Spice said reassuringly, "that is why he is there, to see nonesuch get in this place. Don't you worry, man. All will be well."

Jason hoped so, but he did not feel entirely confident. He decided, however, that there was no use worrying about something which might never happen. He touched the Cap Of Deeper Thinking and held tightly to the Flying Umbrella, and then he felt a little better.

The Petunia Patch was a low-ceilinged room with walls entirely covered in painted petunias: pink, mauve, and purple petunias; frilled petunias and plain petunias; petunia buds and full-blown blossoms. A number of round white tables were scattered about, and mouse waiters were serving tea, coffee, and raspberry-flavored milk. Sitting around the tables, or dancing on the small circular dance floor, was a motley collection of cats, mice, and pigeons. On a raised half-moon platform at the end of the room was the band: two mice playing guitars, two mice singing, two cats playing trumpets, and two cats playing drums. All were dressed in purple velvet jackets with gold epaulettes shining on the shoulders.

Topaz pointed, and excitedly grabbed Strine's shoulder. "Strine, look! Who are they?"

"They're The Purple Petunias," Strine replied, grinning. "The best dance band in the Smaller Animal world. They're starting up now. Want to dance?"

"Yes, *please!*" Topaz cried.

Topaz and Strine went spinning onto the dance floor as the band began playing. Spice asked Calico to dance and, after protesting that she was too old for dancing, Calico finally allowed herself to be persuaded, and proved to be very graceful indeed on the dance floor.

Jason and Oliver sat watching the dancing cats, and after a while, Oliver heaved a sigh.

"I don't wish to appear glum or down-in-the-mouth," he said, "but I do sometimes regret not being able to dance. Trip the light fantastic and all that. When it comes to flying, now, I am second to none. But as far as dancing is concerned, I have an awful feeling that I would be terribly clumsy. Waddling, you know, instead of gliding or whatever one is supposed to do. I'm not even certain I've got any sense of rhythm. And yet, in some strange way, I yearn to dance."

"I know what you mean," Jason said sympathetically. "I feel much the same myself."

At that moment, a pretty girl pigeon came along and noticed Oliver's sad expression.

"What's the matter?" she asked. "I know. You're too shy to try. But you'd really like to dance, wouldn't you?"

"Well . . ." Oliver hesitated. "That is—er—um—I mean to say . . ."

"Come on," the pigeon girl insisted. "It's easy. I'll show you."

So off Oliver went, despite his shyness, and a few moments later Jason was astonished to see a whirl of flailing wings and fluttering feathers flittering madly past. It was Oliver and the little pigeon.

"Hey, Jason!" Oliver shouted. "Look at me! I'm dancing!"

"Splendid," Jason called back. "Wonderful."

All the same, he felt a trifle lonely, left sitting at the table by himself. He ordered a raspberry milk and sipped it slowly through a straw, trying to make it last a long time. He reviewed his situation. Here was The Petunia Patch, just as Joey Blue had directed, but they seemed no nearer than ever to discovering the object of the quest. Jason resolved to ask Strine and Spice if they had ever heard of someone called Perdita, as there didn't seem to be a sign of her anywhere about, and he did not even know who or what she might be. Was she a pigeon? A mouse? At this point Jason could not believe that anyone would ever help him in his search.

"All this journey for nothing," Jason thought, "and in the end I shall have to return to Molanium with nothing changed. Oliver has picked up a little wisdom, although maybe he doesn't realize it yet, and the cats definitely have performed several noble deeds. But what have I done?"

The Purple Petunias had switched to a new tune and, as the two mice singers began, Jason could catch some of the words.

Go, mole, go!

Don't go slow!

Mole? Jason was surprised, for he had seen no moles in The Petunia Patch. Then, all at once, the dancers withdrew to the rim of the floor as a silvery spotlight was focused on the middle. Jason put on his sunglasses so he could see better.

Wonder of wonders! There, dancing into the center of the spotlight, was the most beautiful mole girl he had ever seen. Her fur was a pale golden brown. Around her downy ears she wore a crown of small flowers; pink, white, and yellow. The crowd of cats, mice, and pigeons began to clap and shout.

"Perdita! Per-deet-ah!"

Jason stared. Perdita. Was this indeed Perdita, this enchanting creature? Then Jason remembered. Both Mrs. Weepworthy and Digger O'Bucket had mentioned her name. She was a popular young dancer. But who would ever have thought she would turn out to be one of the molefolk as well?

Perdita danced light as a dandelion, swaying this way and that. Then she motioned to the other dancers, and before long the floor was once again filled and Perdita herself was lost to view. Jason felt he might never see her again. Then he looked up and there she was, standing beside him.

165

"Hello, Jason," she said casually.

"H-how did you know my name?" Jason stammered.

"Oh, easily enough," Perdita said. "Joey Blue sent one of the pigeons to give me a message. Said you were looking for me. What's the matter? Could I do anything to help? What's all this about invisible sickness? The pigeon who carried the message is nice and well-meaning but none too bright. I expect he got Joey's explanation all mixed up. Come on. Tell me what the trouble is."

Jason found that once he had begun talking, it was easy to talk to Perdita. She listened carefully while he told her all about the plight of Molanium, that once-great city, and about the mysterious sickness that had struck it, and about the quest and his now-dwindling hopes of finding a cure for the molefolk.

When he had finished, Perdita shook her head. "I'm dreadfully sorry, Jason," she said, "but I'm afraid I won't be able to help you. I've never heard of a sickness like that."

"Never mind," Jason said, trying not to sound dejected. "I didn't really think you'd be able to help. Thanks for listening, anyway, Perdita."

"Tell me more about Molanium," Perdita said. "It sounds like an odd sort of place."

"Odd?" Jason said. "Why, no, it's not odd. We have a history that dates back to the time of the Romans. It's ever so ancient."

He began to tell Perdita all about the Great Council Hall, and the elders of Molanium, and the Venerable Mole, and how the moles were the keepers of the traditions, so that whatever happened in the dangerous world up Thither, in Molanium things went on as they always had for centuries.

Perdita was looking at him curiously. "Doesn't anything ever *change* in Molanium, Jason?" she asked. "And didn't you ever find life there a little—well—dull? The way you describe it, nothing ever seems to happen. All this devotion to the past. It's all very well, history and all that, but surely new things have to happen, too, don't they? I don't think I'd like to live there. Why, I'd die of boredom."

Jason opened his eyes wide. At the same instant, Pedita opened her eyes wide. They stared at one another. There was a moment's electric silence between them. Then Jason grabbed both Perdita's paws in his.

"That's it!" he cried. "You've hit on the answer, Perdita! I think I've half known it all along, but I'd never have seen it if you hadn't pointed it out. Molanium has been dying of BORE-DOM!"

He *had* half known it all along. Jason remembered now the way he used to feel when he crept out of the Great North Tunnel and went up to the Pink Jungle; the sense of wanting to seek some kind of adventure. He remembered how he had said, after he and the others had encountered Stan the Con Cat, that they must not be *too* careful. They must just take reasonable care and then bash on regardless. It was from that remark that Topaz made up the song *Bash On, Bash On In Majesty.* He recalled, too, his feeling of excitement and discovery, many times on the quest, even when they might be going into danger. He thought of Professor Kingsberry's words to Oliver: "Don't be afraid to change your mind, will you?" Everything had to change and grow. Look at London itself. It was no longer called Londinium, and it must have changed a great deal since the days of the ancient Romans, hundreds of years past. But Molanium had been afraid to change. Jason did not yet have a cure, but he felt he knew at last what had been the cause of the invisible sickness. The molefolk had simply stopped caring about life, because nothing new ever happened any more.

"I've found it!" Jason shouted at the top of his lungs. "Hurrah! Hurrah for Perdita!"

The Purple Petunias again struck up *Go, Mole, Go!* Jason and Perdita began to dance, and Jason found to his amazement that he had unsuspected talents as a dancer.

But, in the very midst of all this joy, there was a stunning crash. The soft purple lights went out. The music stopped. Mice squeaked shrilly in fright. The dancers bumped into one another. Then there was a flash of white glaring light which momentarily blinded all of them, making them blink and painfully close their eyes. From the direction of the doorway came a low growling voice which Jason recognized as that of the Blades' lieutenant, Jacko.

"Quick! We've only got a minute, or they'll be onto us. Grab the brolly and the dolly!"

Jason fumbled for his sunglasses to combat the harsh light, but he had thrown them into the air when he had shouted *Hurrah* a few minutes ago and now could not locate them. He groped for Perdita's paw and could not find it. Then he heard something that chilled his blood. Perdita's voice, screaming for help.

"Perdita!" he cried. "Where are you?"

The cruelly brilliant light went out as abruptly as it had come on. Jason could see again. What he saw frightened him more than he had ever been frightened before. The Petunia Patch was untouched and undamaged by the Blades' raid. But the Flying Umbrella was gone. And, even worse, so was Perdita.

(7)

THE PAD

OF THE GREAT RAT

Perdita captured and the Flying Umbrella stolen. Jason hardly dared think of the awfulness of the situation. The four friends held a quick conference in The Petunia Patch, assisted by Spice and Strine.

Topaz, as usual, was most emotional. "Farewell, Perdita!" she groaned. "Perdita, a long farewell! Kidnapped. Gone forever."

"Stop making such a row," Jason said crossly. "She is *not* gone forever. We must think what to do. Can't you make a sensible suggestion, Topaz, instead of carrying on like that?"

Topaz grew steadier at once. "Find the Great Rat," she advised, "and you'll find Perdita. I'd stake my necklace on that."

"I believe she's right, my dears," Calico said. "It seems likely that the Blades have taken Perdita and the umbrella to their headquarters."

"That's where we'll have to go, then," Jason said decisively.

"If I may for one moment intrude into the conversation," Oliver said, "I'd like to ask just how we are ever going to discover where the Blades' headquarters are? It's all very well to prattle on about finding the Great Rat's base, but it might be anywhere in the whole of London, and London is an extremely large city. Acres and acres. Square mile after square mile. I do not wish to appear discouraging. I do not wish to spread misery and despondency. I only place the question before the assembled company in order to . . ."

"Yes, yes, Oliver," Calico broke in. "We all grasp the point. Has anyone any ideas?"

Jason felt himself seething with impatience, and because this was quite a new sensation to him, he felt dizzy and incapable of clear thinking. All he could think was that they were wasting time in talking, while Perdita was in deadly danger.

"Can't we hurry?" he pleaded. "Can't we *do* something?"

Strine and Spice were looking at each other quizzically.

"Man, you thinking what I thinking?" Spice asked.

"Cobber, the same," Strine replied. "Hampstead Underground. The three-legged rat."

"Tell it, man," Spice said.

"Well, Spice and me," Strine explained, "one day we're walking out of Hampstead Underground station, and who should we see but this creaky old rat? Three-legged, he was. Had a run-in with a trap once, he tells us. He's hobbling along, using a crutch, so Spice and me, we give him a hand, like. Well, we're passing this high old red brick house, just off the High Street, when the old geezer gets very agitated. 'Hurry, please,' he whispers. 'Somebody wicked lives there, and I used to work for him, and it was because of him that I lost me leg, rot him, but if he sees me, I'm done for, for he'll surely set his henchmen on me for having left his service.' So Spice and me, we hustle along with the old fellow, and we got him past the place all right, and off he limps. Now, I have a feeling in my bones that tells me that's the house we're looking for."

"You said it, man," agreed Spice. "You have expressed my own bones' feeling exact. That is the pad of the Great Rat."

"The what?" Jason asked.

"Pad," said Spice. "The hang out. The place where he is dwelling."

"Do you think," Jason said, "that you could find the house again?"

"Certain, man," Spice told him. "We could not be missing it. I see it this minute in my mind-eye."

Oliver began to shake his wings in anticipation of taking off. "Come on, then," he urged. "What are we waiting for?"

Jason snatched the reins around Calico's neck and they were

on their way, Oliver flying ahead and the four cats bounding along as fast as their fleet feet would carry them. First to Earls' Court Station, and onto the underground. *Rattle-rattle-clunk!* Off at Charing Cross and onto a different train, one which would take them to Hampstead. *Kachoink! Kachoink! Kachoink!* The train pounded along, and soon they were there.

"Up the emergency stairs," Strine instructed. "We daren't take the lift or we'll be noticed. There's about a million steps, but it can't be helped."

Finally, panting a little after the long climb, they emerged onto Hampstead High Street, where humans clustered and the lights of restaurants and bookshops and delicatessens winked and beckoned.

"This way," Spice said. "Down the hill, and—mm—let me see. Strine, this the street, man?"

"Yes, this is it," Strine said. "Now only half a block, and—there's the house. Right there."

It was a tall narrow house, joined onto a whole row of similar houses. The red brick of its walls had darkened almost to black over the years, and there was nothing to distinguish it from its neighbors except a large and thick-boughed chestnut tree in the front garden. The friends stood at the gate uncertainly.

"Oliver, I think we need you to go and do some scouting," Jason said. "If this really is the—er—pad of the Great Rat, he and the Blades may be anywhere in the house. We can't all go charging in, or we'd be discovered, and in any event, the front door will undoubtedly be locked."

"Right you are," Oliver said, saluting briskly. "Chief of signals taking off on preliminary survey, sir."

Quickly, but at the same time cautiously, Oliver flew up into the tree boughs and from there to the high pointed roof of the house. The cats and Jason slid like shadows under the gate and hid themselves near the tree, under a broad-leafed hydrangea bush. Before long, Oliver returned.

"They're here, all right," he reported. "I got a brief look into a tiny window at the very top of the house. It's the attic, I would say, so probably the humans hardly ever go there. A dinky little room, it is, quite cramped and low, but there's a door leading somewhere, maybe to another part of the attic. The main thing is, the room I saw was full of Blades."

"What about Perdita?" Jason inquired worriedly.

"Didn't see her," Oliver said. "But I was chatting to a sparrow on the roof, and I learned that a whole gang of Blades turned up here a short time ago with something in a sack. The sack was squirming, he said, as though something was struggling inside it."

"Perdita!" Jason cried. "Come on, we've got to rescue her!"

"How are we going to get in, though?" Calico wondered. "If only the attic window were open."

"It is," Oliver said. "That's how the Blades get in and out. They've got a rope ladder, made of string, actually, and the guard at the top lowers it when any of them want to come in. The sparrow told me."

"That doesn't leave us any better off," Jason said in a disheartened voice.

"Certainly it does," Topaz contradicted. "We cats can climb the tree, Jason, and jump into the attic from one of the top branches. Look, they're quite close to the window."

"What about me, though?" Jason asked. "Could I hang onto your fur, Calico?"

"Pretty risky at that height," Calico said regretfully. "I'd hate to take responsibility for carrying you safely over a leap like that. Couldn't you wait here, my dear?"

"Well . . ." Jason began, but he could not go on.

He felt dreadful. He was, admittedly, terrified at the thought of entering the Great Rat's headquarters. But how much worse to be left here, sitting safely under a hydrangea bush, while the others went in and rescued Perdita.

"Don't worry," Spice was saying to him. "I got a friend who lives in a newspaper shop near here. We are not giving up yet, Jason. I think I know what we need. You wait."

Spice crept out of the garden and shot off towards the newspaper shop. To Jason, the minute seemed like months but, in fact, it was not very long before Spice returned, carrying two objects. One was a ball of heavy string. The other was a mysterious paper bag.

"How do you like this?" he said triumphantly. "With this string we going to make our own rope ladder for you, Jason."

"The very thing!" Oliver cried. "Let's get to work. I'm sure my beak is as sharp as scissors. Now, what lengths would you say, Calico?"

"What's in the paper bag, Spice?" Topaz wanted to know, with her customary curiosity.

Spice winked broadly. "That's my secret weapon," he said. "Every cat should have some little thing up his sleeve."

They all worked furiously, and soon the new rope ladder was complete.

"I think," Jason said, "that I ought to go in alone first. After all, I'm the smallest and least likely to be detected. Then, at my signal, Topaz and Calico can follow. We should keep some reserves outside, just in case. Strine and Spice can keep guard out here, and come in if all of us are captured."

They agreed to this plan, and Oliver flew up with the rope

ladder and hooked it onto a nail on the window ledge. Then Jason began to climb. One rung, two rungs, ten rungs, twenty rungs. The flimsy ladder swayed in the wind and Jason felt that any moment he might be blown off and go plummeting down. He felt weak at this height, but he told himself he must keep on, or Perdita might never be rescued.

At last he gained the window ledge, waved to those below, and jumped into the room, having first checked to make sure no Blades were in sight.

All was still, and the room was apparently deserted now. The floor boards were bare and dirty. Old suitcases and books stood around in dusty piles and stacks. Jason tiptoed across the floor. His scalp was tingling, just under the rim of the Cap Of Deeper Thinking, and this made him even more frightened. Was the cap warning him? If so, what should he do? Where could the Blades be? And where were they keeping Perdita? He took a few more steps and began to explore the room's dark corners, filled with spiderwebs and gauzy blobs of dust. He thought he heard a floor board creaking, and he stopped. Standing perfectly still, he listened. Nothing. He continued.

Then, with no warning at all, something soft fell on him from above. He shrieked, and heard an answering chorus, the familiar tittering he had come to dread so much. The Blades. Jason struggled and found that he was enmeshed in a large butterfly net. Down from the rafters jumped the Blades, boots clanking and knives gleaming. At their head was Jacko, followed by Charlie.

"Clever, aren't you?" Jacko sneered. "Thought you could outwit the Blades, eh? Didn't see why we snatched Perdita, did you? Because we couldn't get all of you at once, that's why. We knew you'd try to rescue her. Now we're going to snare the whole lot of you."

Jason's heart thumped painfully. So he and the others had been lured here, had they? The Great Rat had guessed that somehow they would track down and find his headquarters. It had all been a trap. He, Jason, had walked straight into it, and his friends outside would undoubtedly walk in, too. Not only would they be unable to rescue Perdita. They would not be able to rescue themselves, either.

"Now we're going to leave you alone for a little while," Jacko continued. "A short spell of quiet thinking, you might say."

The Blades immediately followed Jacko through a low door leading to a lighted room which Jason could see only momentarily. He caught an impression of candlelight and rich carpets, then the door slammed and he was by himself, helpless in the butterfly net.

Before he had time to consider his dreadful situation, he

heard a scratching noise. Looking around, he beheld a large and rather fat mole. The mole sidled secretively towards Jason.

"Sh . . ." he whispered. "Not a word."

"Who are you?" Jason asked in amazement. "Why, I never thought I'd see another mole here, except Perdita, of course. Are you a prisoner, too, sir?"

"Indeed I am," the plump mole said sorrowfully. "They're not keeping me in a net any more because they know only too well I can't escape. It's a horrible life, to be a prisoner. You can't imagine how I long for the smell of the earth."

"How awful for you," Jason sympathized. "How long have you been here?"

"Six months," the plump mole said in a doleful voice. "But I've been thinking a lot and I'm rapidly coming to a conclusion."

"What's that, sir?" Jason wanted to know.

"The Great Rat and the Blades," the plump mole said, "only want one simple thing from any of us. That is for us to go home and leave their territory alone. Personally, I think this may prove to be the wisest course. Live and let live. I'm thinking of telling them of my decision tonight. Perhaps we could talk about it, you and I. We might even approach them together. Moral support, you know."

Jason began to feel suspicious. How was it, he asked himself, that the mole was still so plump after six months' imprisonment by the Blades? How was it that his decision had coincided so neatly with Jason's capture? Yet, at the same time, Jason desperately wanted to believe that the mole was a friend in need, an ally. Maybe he was only imagining things about the plump mole. Nevertheless, he decided to stand his ground.

"This city is not the Blades' territory," he said. "They're a gang of criminals. They bully as many of the Smaller Animals as they can, and get them to pay for so-called protection against each other. But it's really the Blades that all these animals have to fear the most. Anyway, I'm not going home until I've rescued Perdita."

"No doubt that could be arranged," the plump mole suggested. "Maybe the Great Rat would agree to my taking Perdita back to her home if you and the others agreed to leave London and never return."

"Just who *are* you?" Jason inquired, his suspicions now growing. "At one time I would have taken for granted that I could trust you because you're a mole. But not any longer. Did the Great Rat by any chance think you could persuade me to give up the quest and go meekly home?"

"Tut, tut, my dear boy, how can you possibly think such a thing?" the plump mole said, smiling winningly.

"I don't know what you're after," Jason said staunchly. "But I refuse to go back to Molanium until I'm ready to go, and

I refuse to leave this house unless Perdita comes with me. So go and tell that to whoever sent you here."

The plump mole's smile faded and his eyes grew narrow and mean.

"Little fool," he spat out. "You'll be sorry."

With that, he scuttled away. There was utter silence for a few minutes, and then the door opened, and six Blades marched in, each bearing a lighted candle, which they set in holders about the room. This advance guard was followed by a strange procession. A corps of Blades entered, each pulling a short silken cord, and attached to the cords was a kind of throne on wheels. The throne was painted silver, and the high back of it was embossed with a large silver B on a shield of black. On the throne was an enormously fat rat with long dark whiskers and small reddish eyes. He was clad in a long loose robe of black brocade, embroidered with silver blades. His paws were covered with jeweled rings. Under one arm he carried Jason's Flying Umbrella.

"Ah, Jason," the Great Rat said in a cruel voice. "What a pleasure to meet you at long last. I see you have not been impressed with my faithful mole servant, whom I sent here in the hope that he might make you listen to reason."

Jason said nothing. *When in doubt, keep your mouth shut,* he told himself. He was quaking inside the butterfly net, but he hoped no one would notice.

"Now, my dear fellow," the Great Rat went on in his softly evil voice, "I do suggest that you would have been well advised to strike a bargain with me. Now it is too late. I'm afraid I shall have to get my Blades to deal with you. In a rather nasty way. Our usual method is to tie the—ah—awkward one into a weighted sack and drop him into whatever water happens to be nearest—in this case, Hampstead Ponds."

Jason wanted to cry, *what have you done with Perdita?* But he knew it would be no use, so he still made no reply.

"You see, Jason," the Great Rat continued, "we do not like creatures like you, full of hope and the joys of spring, questing for cures and suchlike. No, no, that won't do at all. Nor do I like you and your friends opposing my Blades, as you did at Marylebone Station. I expect instant agreement with my commands. When the Great Rat speaks, all the world trembles and bows down in fear!"

He puffed out his chest pridefully with these words, and all the Blades bowed low and chanted. *Hail, the Leader! Hail the Great Rat!*

"You see?" the Great Rat said, with a satisfied smirk. "My faithful followers."

He turned to the nearest Blade. "Bring in the mole girl."

Perdita! Jason's heart gave a leap. At least she was still alive. The Blades trundled Perdita in on a low wheelbarrow and dumped her on the floor beside Jason. She, too, was encased in a butterfly net.

"Oh, Jason," she whispered. "So they've caught you, as well."

"Don't give up," Jason tried to comfort her. "The others are . . ."

At that moment, he looked towards the window. There, on the topmost branches of the tree, were Calico and Topaz, stealthily waiting. Jason wanted to warn them for, near the window, inside the room, stood a massed brigade of Blades, holding butterfly nets ready. The Blades had not yet seen the cats, but if the cats jumped in the window, the nets would be flung over them. Jason decided that he must warn the cats, even if it meant that he and Perdita could never be rescued. But just as he was about to call out to them, there was an abrupt sound, the grating sound of wood against wood.

The trapdoor which led from the house into the attic was being shoved open.

"Humans!" gasped the Great Rat in a strangled voice. "Quick—out of sight!"

But it was not humans. Before even one Blade had time to move as much as a muscle, in burst Strine and Spice.

"Arr!" yowled Strine.

"Rrrow!" screeched Spice.

In their paws they were carrying a large number of short thin sticks with bits of string on the end, and to these bits of string they were rapidly touching the flames of matches. Jason stared.

Spice's secret weapon. Fireworks!

The black cat and the ginger cat threw the lighted fireworks directly at the Blades and the Great Rat. The fireworks sputtered and crackled and exploded everywhere. At this signal, Calico and Topaz soared in through the window and joined the fray.

The scene that followed was wild. Mice and rats scampering madly about, falling over one another in their frenzied efforts to escape. Fireworks blaring and shooting off sparks. Cries of *Dynamite!* and *We're being blown sky-high!* from the ranks of Blades. The cats fighting in all directions at once. Strine yelling his battle cry—*From Australia, with love!*—as he bonked two rats' heads together. Spice roaring *Man, man, this fiercer than a cricket match!* as he knocked four Blades into a corner. Topaz and Calico steadily fighting their way to Jason and Perdita, until they had succeeded in freeing the moles. Then Jason glanced towards the window.

"Quick! The Great Rat is escaping!"

Sure enough, there on the window ledge stood the Great Rat. In one paw he held Jason's Flying Umbrella. He had opened it, and was desperately twiddling with the controls. Then

he grasped how the thing worked, and a thin, knifelike smile crossed his puffy face. He was just about to switch on the umbrella and fly away, when down from the roof swooped none other than Oliver. With a sharp darting movement, Oliver snatched the Flying Umbrella in his beak and carried it off.

The Great Rat began to quiver and shake. Then he crawled

along the window ledge towards the drainpipe. The effect upon his followers was stunning.

"Look!" a Blade shouted. "He's leaving! The Leader! The G.R.! He's running away! It can't be possible!"

But it was. The Great Rat was deserting his followers in an attempt to save his own skin. The Blades stared. Was this the leader who had proclaimed himself to be so mighty? Was this the creature they had so blindly followed? Now he was revealed for the flabby coward he really was. A low growl arose from the Blades, rising to loud angry cries. *Boo to him, the traitor! Fine Leader he turned out to be!*

Jacko, who had always rather fancied himself as leader of the Blades, seized the opportunity. "Down with the Great Rat!" he cried.

Now the stupid Blades followed Jacko just as blindly as they had once followed the Great Rat. Those who had not been sent spinning into corners by the cats began to rush towards the window, pushing and shrieking. In the hubbub, the last cry of the Great Rat was lost. There was a dreadful thud outside, and then silence. The Blades peered out.

"What's happened?" Perdita whispered to Jason.

Jason covered her eyes with his paw. "Don't look," he said. "They've shoved him off the drainpipe and he's crashed down. I believe the Great Rat is dead."

And so he was. The proud and evil rat had fallen and met his end. The Great Rat was finished forever. When they saw what they had done, the Blades became jittery. Even Jacko lost his nerve. All they wanted now was to get away as fast as possible. Forgetting those of their group who still lay bruised on the floor, the remaining Blades slithered down the drainpipe and ran off, through hedges and into alleys, back to the dark sewers where no one would find them.

Oliver flew back and came in the window. He handed the Flying Umbrella to Jason. "Yours, I believe?" he said nonchalantly.

"Oh, Oliver," said Jason, "how can I ever thank you?"

"No need," Oliver replied. "Well, it looks as though we've won. The Blades have scattered, and the Great Rat will never bother anyone again."

Jason could see Perdita trembling slightly. No wonder, after this evening. He reached out for her paw and held it tightly. For a few seconds no one spoke.

"How did you manage to get in?" Jason finally asked Strine and Spice.

"Sheer luck," Strine said. "Human came in the front door, and Spice and me nipped in behind him."

Just then, they all heard human voices from below.

"Giles," a woman's voice was imploring, "can't you for pity's sake go and *see*? I'm sure something has *exploded* up there. I heard the oddest noises."

A grumpy man-voice grumbled agreement, indicating that Giles would soon be appearing in the attic. The friends looked at one another.

"Back to The Petunia Patch, on the double!" Strine advised.

"The fight may be over, but if we get nabbed by those humans, in their attic, I wouldn't give tuppence for our chances."

The way out was easy. Before Giles could climb the ladder up to the attic, the friends were out and away.

At last they were in The Petunia Patch again, sipping hot milk and discussing the night's events.

"Just think," Jason mused. "The Great Rat dead, and the Blades' whole gang broken up. I can hardly believe it."

"Yeh, that's the end of the Blades, for sure," Strine said. "At least, until the next time."

"What do you mean, the next time?" Jason asked, dismayed.

"He means no battle is fought once and for all," Spice said, shrugging. "Don't you worry about that, Jason, man. You fight your battle here and now, one by one. Nothing going to get settled for all time, you know."

Jason pondered. "It's a little like Molanium," he said. "The molefolk thought they had everything nicely settled, once and for all. But they didn't. I guess it's like Spice says—all you can do is what needs to be done right here and now."

Then he realized they were all looking at him—Strine, Spice, Calico, Topaz, Oliver, and most of all, Perdita.

"I don't express myself terribly well," Jason stammered. "Not like you, Oliver."

"Piff," Topaz commented. "Oliver doesn't express himself that well. He just opens his mouth and a whole lot of words come tumbling out, that's all."

"If I were as ridiculously conceited as you are, Topaz," Oliver said huffily, "I would think twice before criticizing any-one else."

"Now, now, my dears," Calico soothed. "Both of you hush up. The captain's not finished what he had to say."

Jason smiled inwardly. The turmoil of the evening was over, and they were all getting back to normal.

"I've forgotten what else I was going to say," he admitted. "I can only think of one thing I really want to speak about."

"What's that?" they all wanted to know.

Jason turned to Perdita, who was sitting beside him.

"Perdita, would you . . ." he began. "That is, do you think you ever could . . . I mean to say, I know it must be exciting to live here and be a dancer, and maybe you'd find the country rather quiet, but I do think you're the most wonderful . . ."

"If you're trying to say would I marry you," Perdita said in her direct way, "then the answer is *Yes*. Oh, yes, Jason. Of course. I've been wondering when you were going to ask."

Then the jubilation really began. The Purple Petunias

191

began to play *Go, Mole, Go!* The guitars twanged, the trombones tooted, the drums bonged and boomed, and the mice singers sang until their throats were sore.

And everyone danced until dawn.

(8)

THE DRUMS OF THE NIGHT, THE TRUMPETS OF THE DAY

Everything was arranged. Perdita had said good-by to her parents, and she and Jason had promised to come back soon on a visit. Now it was good-by at The Petunia Patch.

"You will come and see us, won't you?" Topaz said rather tearfully to Strine and Spice.

" 'Course we will," Strine said. "Won't we, cobber?"

"You said it, man," Spice agreed. "We going to ask one truck cat we know, and get a lift with him."

"You'll always be welcome," Calico said, speaking for all of them, "and we'll come back to visit The Petunia Patch, too, just as soon as we can."

There was a flurry from the bandstand, and the Purple Petunias in their velvet jackets were walking in a group towards

Jason and the others. They stood there, shuffling their feet and whispering among themselves. *You do the talking. No, you. Not me, you twit, you.* Finally one of the mouse singers stepped forward and spoke.

"Us boys—that is, all of us Purple Petunias—we thought we'd like to give you some little souvenir to remember us by. So this is for Topaz—"

It was a pair of earrings, pale purple and shaped like petunias.

"Oh, they're lovely!" Topaz exclaimed in pleasure. "Shall I put them on right now? Don't they go beautifully with my necklace? Don't I look glamorous? Thanks a trillion times."

The mouse singer drew something else out of the paper bag at his feet. A purple velvet neck bow with a large velvet petunia on it. This was for Calico.

"It's truly elegant, my dears," Calico said. "I shall wear it always."

For Oliver there was a velvet jacket, exactly the same as those of the Purple Petunias themselves, with gold epaulettes on the shoulders.

"Wait until my Gran sees this," Oliver chirped excitedly. "She'll hardly recognize me, I'll be so splendid. I can see it all now. Me, flitting from tree to tree at home, not the slightest bit boastful, you understand, but recognized by one and all as a model of owlish fashion. Oh, I must really watch it, or I'll be as vain as Topaz."

"Piff to you," Topaz said affectionately. "You're far worse than I am, Oliver, already."

Then the Petunias handed to Jason the most wonderful gift imaginable—three mole-size drums and three small silver trumpets.

"These are the Drums of The Night," they explained, "and these are the Trumpets Of The Day. We had them made specially for you, Jason. They're to remember us by, but they're also for luck. As long as these drums and trumpets sound, the molefolk will never forget your quest and what you taught them about the cure for the invisible sickness."

"Thank you very, very much," Jason said gratefully. "I'll guard the drums and trumpets well. But I'm not sure yet, myself, what I'll be able to tell the molefolk about the cure for the invisible sickness. All I know is that things have to change."

"Don't worrry," one of the cat drummers said confidently. "When it really comes to it, you'll find you know what to say and do."

"I—well, I'll try," Jason said, repeating his old motto.

"Who could say more?" the Purple Petunias said in a chorus. "Good luck, Jason!"

"We'll never forget you," Jason said. "Will we, Perdita?"

195

"We certainly won't," Perdita agreed. "But we mustn't feel sad about going, Jason. We'll see all of them again. And we can write letters."

At this, the mouse singer who had passed out the presents suddenly gasped. "My heavens!" he cried. "We nearly forgot! Where is it, boys?"

There were murmurs of *I thought you had it* and *No, I gave it to you to hold, don't you remember?* Finally someone found what they were looking for—a neat little parcel done up in silver paper. This they handed to Perdita.

"A present for me, too?" she said. "I wasn't expecting anything. I knew about the things for Jason and the others, but I never thought—oh, what's in this box?"

She quickly took off the silver paper, and there in a blue leather box was one half of a miniature walkie-talkie set. The Purple Petunias explained gleefully that they had the other half of the highly powerful set, so Perdita could tune in any time and talk to friends at The Petunia Patch.

"It's so you won't get homesick," the mouse singer added.

Perdita was very touched by such a thoughtful gift. "I'll cherish it," she said. "And I'll tune in every weekend and have a chat with all of you."

Now the time had come to depart. With a last farewell and a waving of paws, the members of the quest set off for home.

All went well for a while. They managed to get a lift on a truck, and within a few hours they were out of London and into the countryside once more. Then the five friends had to turn off onto a smaller road which would lead them back the way they had come, so they left the truck and continued by foot and wing.

They were loping along pleasantly, enjoying the smell of the earth, the mild evening air, and the first glimmering of stars, when Oliver, who had been hovering above them, gave a shriek of alarm.

"Halt! Wait a second! Jason! It can't be true. But it is. We're being followed. It's the Blades again."

Shocked and horrified, they all looked behind them, and sure enough, there were the last of the Blades, grim and harsh-faced, led by the wicked mouse lieutenant, Jacko. They were marching along steadily, their black boots snickering on the road, their knives shining evilly.

"Run!" Calico shouted. "It's our only chance. Head off the lane and through the fields. We may lose them that way."

With Jason clinging to Calico's fur, Perdita clinging to Topaz, and Oliver fluttering in the air above, the friends sped across a meadow, through the tall grass and the wild buttercups. But the Blades continued to pursue them. Faster and faster ran

197

the friends. Faster and faster ran the Blades, until Jason, glancing back, could see Jacko's crooked smile. Just then they saw a river ahead.

"Whatever shall we do?" moaned Topaz. "Look at that. It's so wide I doubt if I could leap it at all, much less with Perdita on my back!"

"Quick! Perdita!" Jason cried. "It's the flying Umbrella for you and me. Oliver's all right, and the cats will have to jump across."

"Don't know if I can, my dear," Calico said uncertainly. "That river looks as wide as a house."

"You *must*," Jason implored. "You've got to!"

"Well," Calico said, "as you've so often remarked, Jason, *I will try*."

They reached the river's edge. Hurriedly, Jason put up the Flying Umbrella. He and Perdita both grabbed hold of the handle, and Jason turned the *Onward* and *Upward* knobs. Closer and closer cantered the Blades, their sharp yellow teeth ready to attack.

The Blades were almost upon the group of friends when the Flying Umbrella took off—up—up—up. Jason and Perdita sailed gracefully through the air and across the river. At the same moment, both the cats took a gigantic leap and just managed to clear the river, landing in a heap on the opposite side. Oliver, after making sure that his friends were safely across, did one last pirouette in the air above the Blades' heads, and flew swiftly over to join the others.

The Blades could not follow. There was no way they could get across the river.

"Can't you swim?" Jacko kept snarling at them. "Why can't you? You should be able to. Here, jump in and have a go. Come on, you Blades. Hop to it! Don't forget I'm the leader now!"

But the Blades would not obey. They burst into rebellious cries. *Don't see you swimming, Jacko, do we? C'mon, boys, he's just like the Great Rat. Wants us to take all the chances, not him. Who's for home? Me, for one.*

The five friends watched from the other bank of the river. Jacko, gnashing his teeth with fury, was trying to gather his gang together and prevent them from straggling off in ones and twos.

Just then, a clear piercing whistle sounded, and a familiar shape bounded into view a short distance from the Blades, followed by several unfamiliar shapes.

"Why, it's P. C. Wattles!" Jason cried.

"And what's more," Oliver shouted, "he's got the Force with him!"

Sure enough, it was P. C. Wattles, accompanied by four other police cats. Before Jacko and the remaining Blades had time to realize what was happening, they found themselves

199

tightly handcuffed and guarded. Only then did P. C. Wattles turn and call a greeting across the river to his old friends.

"Hi, there!" he said in his cheery voice. "Guess you won't need to be worrying about the Blades any more. Take 'em into custody, we will. We've got the rest already."

"My goodness, it's good to see you, Constable," Calico said in a heartfelt tone. "But how did you ever guess the Blades would be here?"

P. C. Wattles winked. "Well, to tell you the truth, ma'am," he replied, "it was partly due to Stan the Con Cat. Yes, Winstanley decided to tell us all he knew, hoping we'd let him off easy, see? Crooked to the last, old Stan, not that it'll do him any good. One of my mates followed the trail in London, and your pals Strine and Spice very kindly put us on the right track by showing us which way you'd gone. After that, it was simple logic."

"I think it was just marvelous," Topaz purred admiringly.

They said good-by to P. C. Wattles and the other police cats, and began again on the journey home.

"I have a feeling," Jason said, "that we have encountered our last peril on the quest."

"It's been a good quest, hasn't it?" Topaz remarked. "Don't you think so, Jason?"

"Yes," Jason said, "and you and Calico did what you set out to do. You definitely did many noble deeds."

"Perhaps we did a few," Calico said modestly. "You remember, though, we wanted to prove that the catfolk were all fine and good? Well, somehow that doesn't seem quite so important now. We've met good cats and bad on this journey. I suppose there will always be some of both. That's a useful thing to know."

Oliver was rustling his wings nervously. "Look here . . ." he cried. "I've just realized—I mean, I know I'm not very wise and all that, but it has just come to me in a sort of flash—something we've all found out on the quest. We've met cats, moles, owls, and mice of all sorts, haven't we? Some real shockers like Stan the Con Cat, or the Blades, or those silly owls, Ugh, Brr, and Phew, or that creepy old mole that Jason ran into at the Great Rat's headquarters. But there were all the friendly and helpful ones, too: P. C. Wattles, and Mrs. Weepworthy, and Digger

O'Bucket, and the nightwatch cat, and Madame Amina, and Strine and Spice, and Professor Kingsberry, and most of all, Perdita. I mean to say—well—maybe this doesn't sound too profound, but it seems to me there's good and bad in all tribes. It's your friends who count. And we've all stayed friends and met quite a few new ones, haven't we?"

"Good for you, Oliver," Jason said approvingly. "You've expressed it very well."

"You see, my dear?" Calico said warmly. "It's just as Professor Kingsberry told you: you've learned more than you realized."

"Oh, well," Oliver said rather bashfully, "I don't know about that. But at least I'm not trying to be the wisest owl ever, any more, so perhaps that's a beginning. Don't suppose I shall ever learn how to keep quiet, though."

"Please don't," Perdita said, smiling. "We like you just as you are, Oliver."

"Really?" Oliver said. "That's the nicest thing I've heard in ages."

Calico turned to Jason. "What about you, Captain?" she said. "You found what you were looking for, the cause of the invisible sickness, and now it'll be up to you and Perdita to help the molefolk with a cure. But I believe you've found out something else as well."

"What could that be?" Jason asked, mystified.

"I think you've discovered," Calico said gently, "that you can act more bravely than you may feel."

Jason's prediction proved to be correct. They met no more perils, and early the following evening they were home again.

The cats went scooting back into the house, anxious to see their humans once more. Oliver put on his new velvet jacket and flew up high into the big elm tree where his Gran lived. And Jason and Perdita, hand in hand, made their way down the Great North Tunnel to Molanium.

What a rejoicing there was in the mole city. Jason's mother, Calpurnia, wept with gladness to see her son back home safely. His three sisters, Grace, Beauty, and Faith, danced for joy, and the entire family, including uncles and cousins, welcomed Perdita into their midst. Then they all went to the Council Hall to meet the Elders and the Venerable Mole. Jason felt a little anxious, for all the molefolk had gathered and were waiting to hear what he had to say.

The Venerable Mole placed both his paws on Jason's shoulders for an instant. "My boy, it is good to see you again," he said. "Dare we hope that you have found a cure for Molanium's invisible sickness?"

Jason swallowed hard and said *Courage, courage* several times to himself.

"I—I think, sir," he began. "That is, it was really Perdita who hit on the answer. As soon as she said it, I could see it was true. You see, we've been living too much in the past. Nothing interesting going on now. Everything just the same for hundreds of years. Monotony. Everyone sort of lost heart, without realizing it. Sir, elders, and molefolk, that was the invisible sickness—boredom!"

Jason wondered if he had said too much or not enough. Beside him, Perdita applauded loyaly. But what would the Venerable Mole say? What would the molefolk in general say?

Suddenly, and astonishingly, there was a great cheer, and everyone in the Council Hall was on his feet, applauding and shouting. The younger moles stamped their feet and clapped their paws enthusiastically, and even the older moles seemed approving.

Then Jason remembered something important. Reaching up his paws, he removed the Cap Of Deeper Thinking from his head and handed it back to the Venerable Mole. The Venerable Mole held up a paw for silence.

"Jason," he said solemnly, "I want you to take back the Cap Of Deeper Thinking. It is now yours. You have earned it. I have a feeling that you and Perdita are right. I have been Venerable

205

Mole in Molanium for a long time. Now, being a very old mole indeed, I should like to retire. If the elders and molefolk agree, I should like you to take my place."

Cheers rose from the molefolk, and shouts of *Hurrah for Jason! Hurrah for the old Venerable! Hurrah for both!* Jason hardly knew what to say.

"Thank you, sir," he said at last. "If you want it that way, then I will try. But I couldn't do it alone. Couldn't we have a council that was half composed of the Elders and half composed of—as you might say—the youngers?"

"I see no reason why not," the Venerable Mole said gravely.

Something else was bothering Jason. "Sir," he said, "I think of you as the Venerable Mole, and I'm sure all the others do, as well. Even if you are retired, couldn't you keep that title? I would much prefer to be known simply as Mayor."

The Venerable Mole nodded his head in agreement, and the molefolk cried *Hurrah for Jason, Mayor of Molanium!*

But still things did not seem quite straight to Jason. "I'm sorry to go on and on," he said, addressing the crowd, "but it appears to me that the first change should be the name of our city. Molanium was a good name in ancient times. But does it really belong here and now? Our city is not, as we once thought, the center of the world. There are other mole cities, too. Ours is just one among many, although it is much loved by us because it's ours. Couldn't we call it by some simpler name? I suggest Mole-ville."

There was a lot of whispering and scratching of heads, and Jason wondered if he had done the right thing. After all, many of the molefolk would be deeply attached to the old name. Finally it was decided to take a vote. The Venerable Mole counted the show of paws.

"The Ayes have it," he announced. "Henceforth, our city will be known as Moleville, and may the new name bring us luck."

"What about the molefolk motto?" a voice shouted from the crowd. *"Festina lente!* Hasten slowly! That doesn't seem much in keeping with new eras and all that."

Jason was perplexed. He turned to Perdita. "I can't seem to think of a thing," he confessed. "Have you got any ideas? I keep remembering that time on the quest when I felt we ought to take reasonable care and then bash on regardless, and Topaz made up the song about it. But I don't really believe *Bash On* would be a very suitable motto, do you?"

Perdita thought for a moment. "What about this?" she said at last. *"Take A Care, Then Do And Dare."*

Thus it was that the newly named town of Moleville received its new motto and began a new lease on life. The tunnel building was resumed, and before long the diggers of Moleville discovered that they had dug all the way through to half a dozen other mole villages and towns. A small railway was installed, entirely constructed by young moles who were keen on engines and the like, and the folk from Moleville began visiting moles in other places and finding out how they lived. Sports Evenings were held, at which moles from all the towns met and held wrestling matches and digging contests. A few mole lads, as it turned out, were extremely interested in going off and exploring such places as the Pink Jungle, and these adventurous young moles drew maps of the territory, and even went so far as to search for buried treasure. Among the things they found were several old coins, a beautifully painted blue tile, and many fine fragments of china and glass. These were put on display at the newly built Moleville Museum. Under-earth gardens were begun, and the members of the Moleville Gardeners' Association met twice a month to compare the best ways of growing ferns, miniature trees and wild flowers by having airshafts that would catch the sunlight and pipe it down to the plants, which needed it. The molefolks' eyes, of course, were bothered by sunlight but, as the sunshaft procedure naturally took place during the days, when the moles were asleep, the gardens flourished without proving troublesome.

A small but brainy group of mole scientists began a research program known as M.I.S., Moles In Space, and at the fourteenth try, they managed to launch a rocket as far as the top of the tallest beech tree on the plains of Thither. Unfortunately, the two moles who had gone with the rocket got stuck on the tree boughs, and Jason had to go and rescue them with the Flying Umbrella, but the scientists were not discouraged. The next attempt, they vowed, would be a complete success, and Jason believed it would be, for the space moles were very determined and had endless enthusiasm for their work.

Perdita started a kindergarten for mole youngsters, where they all made up stories and danced and did satisfyingly sloppy things such as paw painting or, as Perdita put it, "Squooshing about with colors." Jason was kept quite busy being Mayor, but not too busy to be able to start his own project, which was a kind of travel agency called Molytours. Trips to London were started, with Strine and Spice conducting the visitors around and showing them the sights. Digger O'Bucket and Mrs. Weepworthy (who was now Mrs. O'Bucket) began a mole hotel by extending the cottage at Leicester Square underground station, and the folk from Moleville always stayed there, for the prices were reasonable, the food excellent, and the songs free. Jason hoped in time to extend his tours to other countries as well, and was carrying on a correspondence with moles in Italy, America, and

North Africa, to see what could be arranged. He had a remarkable postal service, for Oliver took his letters airmail as far as London, and Joey Blue the pigeon then took them airmail as far as the coast, where he handed them over to several sea gull friends, who speedily delivered them airmail to their destination.

At the onset of dusk in Moleville, the Drums of The Night were heard, played by young moles trained by Perdita and Jason, and at the beginning of dawn, the Trumpets of The Day sounded their silvery notes, telling the molefolk that the night's work was over. As well as this, however, the drums and trumpets played gaily in a club known as The Underground. The name of the club had been picked by Jason, as it reminded him of London, and the walls were decorated with the blue and scarlet designs which brought back memories of the quest.

Everyone was too busy, working and playing and exploring, to worry about any kind of ailment and so, almost without anyone's realizing it, the invisible sickness disappeared.

"What was the best thing you found on the quest, Jason?" Perdita asked one evening. "Apart from the cure for the city, I mean."

Jason did not have to think very long. "You," he said.

Perdita smiled tenderly. "I thought you'd say that," she admitted, "or I wouldn't have asked."

The friends still meet under the rhododendron bush, near the Pink Jungle. Some night, you might be passing by, and you might hear what you imagine to be only a couple of cats meowing into the darkness, only an owl hooting, only the squeak of several Smaller Animals which might be moles. But what you would really be hearing is the song of the friends who went together on a quest. Topaz, because she could make up verses, was the one who brought their old song up to date, in order to include Perdita. So, if some evening you should chance to hear the mingled voices of cats, moles, and owl, this is the song they will be singing:

Five for One, and One for Five,
Together, long as we're alive!

A Note About the Author

MARGARET LAURENCE's Knopf adult novels have been highly praised, her most outstanding work being *A Jest of God* which was made into the award-winning film, *Rachael, Rachael*. Mrs. Laurence is presently a writer-in-residence at the University of Toronto. *Jason's Quest* is her first juvenile novel.

A Note on the Type

The text of this book has been set on the Linotype in a type face called "Baskerville." The face is a facsimile reproduction of type cast from molds made for John Baskerville (1706–1775) from his designs. The punches for the revived Linotype Baskerville were cut under the supervision of the English printer, George W. Jones.

John Baskerville's original face was one of the forerunners of the type-style known as "modern face" to printers: a "modern" of the period of 1800.

This book was composed by The Book Press, Brattleboro, Vt.; printed by Universal Lithographers, Inc., Timonium, Md.; and bound by L. H. Jenkins, Inc., Richmond, Va. Typography by Cynthia Krupat.